THE BAKER STREET BOYS

If Mr. Sherlock Holmes had been in the country when the Baker Street Irregulars stumbled across the mystery of the Captive Clairvoyant, then no doubt he would have given immediate assistance.

But Mr. Holmes was in Switzerland engaged in a deadly duel of wits with his most feared opponent, the evil Professor Moriarty; and so the Baker Street Irregulars, the gang of ragamuffins who sometimes assisted Mr. Holmes in his investigations, had to rely on their own wits.

It all began—and ended—in Trump's Music Hall, the theatre where Sparrow was employed, where the star of the show was The Amazing Marvin, Hypnotist Extraordinaire and Mentalist Supreme! But Marvin had a secret and sinister agenda....

Two marvelous tales of Holmesiana!

Borgo Press Books by BRIAN BALL

The Baker Street Boys: Two Baker Street Irregulars Novellas
The Evil at Monteine: A Novel of Horror (Ruane #2)
Mark of the Beast: A Novel of Horror (Ruane #1)

THE BAKER STREET BOYS

TWO BAKER STREET IRREGULARS NOVELLAS

BRIAN BALL

Based on a Television Series by Anthony Read

THE BORGO PRESS

MMXII

THE BAKER STREET BOYS

FIRST BORGO PRESS EDITION

Published by Wildside Press LLC

www.wildsidebooks.com

DEDICATION

For Elisabeth

CONTENTS

THE CASE OF THE CAPTIVE CLAIRVOYANT

CHAPTER ONE

If Mr. Sherlock Holmes had been in the country when the Baker Street Irregulars stumbled across the mystery which I have called "The Case of the Captive Clairvoyant," then no doubt he would have given immediate assistance.

But Mr. Holmes was in Switzerland engaged in a deadly duel of wits with his most feared opponent, the evil Professor Moriarty; and so the Baker Street Irregulars, the gang of ragamuffins who sometimes assisted Mr. Holmes in his investigations, had to rely on their own wits. I, Sergeant Hopkins, had taken it upon myself to record the investigations in which the great Sherlock Holmes was employed to only a limited extent— those not described by Dr. Watson.

It all began—and ended—in the theatre where Sparrow was employed, Trump's Music-hall.

That week there was a mixed bag of acts. There was Signor Maccarelli, who threw knives; Gorgeous Gertie, who sang sentimental ballads, Madame Pompadour the comedienne; and a magician; but the star of the show was The Amazing Marvin, as he was described. "Marvel at the Mystic Powers of Marvin," so the poster invited passers-by: "Hypnotist Extraordinary! Mentalist Supreme!"

"Ah, excellent!" beamed Mr. Trump to Bert the doorman as he saw the packed house. "Marvin's still bringing them in. Another week of this and who knows—I could get him to play to royalty!" And he clicked his heels as he rocked backwards and forwards with satisfaction.

"Marvin's good," agreed Bert. "Sparrow!" he yelled. "Placards for Mr. Marvin—he's on in fifteen minutes!"

"Right, Bert!" called Sparrow.

"Get me a drink!" yelled a large lady from one of the dressing-rooms. "Be quick, Sparrow, darling!"

Sparrow sometimes thought he needed three sets of legs and hands. He was a general dogs-body for the artistes, as well as a sweeper-up and an assistant scene-changer, but his principal job was to make sure that the placards which announced each act were properly displayed on the stage before the artistes began their acts.

"Gin and polly coming up!" he cried to Madame Pompadour, who was in need of a drink before her act. "I got the placards ready, Bert!" he yelled back to the doorman.

"How's the new boy shaping up, Bert?" Mr. Trump asked.

"Sparrow?" said Bert. "He's a good lad, very obliging and quick, and he's popular with the artistes, especially young Mary."

"Is that so?" Mr. Trump said, frowning.

"I'll tell him to keep away from her if you like, sir," said Bert, anxious to oblige his employer.

"No, don't do that," said Mr. Trump. "He isn't doing any harm. Anyway," he said, catching sight of the small figures "she might need cheering up."

Bert saw the small pale face of the girl, whose bright red dress emphasised her pallor. Then Bert looked at her huge, staring eyes.

"No," agreed Bert, swallowing nervously. "She do stare so, don't she, Mr. Trump?"

Mr. Trump shrugged.

"Marvin needs her in the act—but she's a trouper and she's got to bear up. The theatre's a hard place, Bert, but it's our living and Marvin's and the girl's too. But you can let the boy talk to her. And Bert," he added.

"Yessir?"

"Let me know if he hears anything interesting from her, will you?"

"Such as what, Mr. Trump?"

"Oh, little things, you know. Nothing special—I just feel rather concerned for her. But you'll remember what I said?"

"You can rely on me, Mr. Trump," said Bert as Mr. Trump went to the front of the house. "Now, what does Sparrow talk to her about?"

Sparrow was listening, not talking; and as he listened he realised that Mary was the unhappiest girl he had ever known. He hadn't sought her out that evening—by chance he heard her sobbing in a darkened doorway where she had gone to hide her tears. And, so it seemed, from Marvin.

"He's getting ready for the act," she told him. "He'll call me soon—and I sometimes think I shall go out of my mind when he sends for me!" Sparrow had spoken to Mary on a dozen occasions, but no hint of her mental torment had come out before tonight. He was totally perplexed now, for there seemed to be no reason for her misery.

"It isn't all that bad," said Sparrow. "Cheer up, Mary!" But her sobs shook her body.

"No one knows what it's like, being with Marvin!" she sobbed. "He puts on a kind face when there's anyone around, but I think he really hates me!"

"But he can't!" said Sparrow in astonishment. "He's your dad!"

"He's not, he's my stepfather, and my name's Mary Ashley, and I've been with him for only a few months—he met and married my mother in New York and learned the act from her, then she died almost as soon as he learned the routines. And he keeps me because he needs me, but he's cruel, terribly cruel!"

"I can't say as how I likes him much," said Sparrow. "He's got a nasty look about him."

"He's evil! I know it!" cried Mary Marvin.

"'S'trewth!" said Sparrow. "It is bad, ain't it?"

"I wish with all my heart I could get away from him!" the girl cried, and Sparrow was shocked by the force of her feelings.

"Well, I should leave him!" he declared.

"Leave him?" said the girl slowly, and her great eyes stared back at Sparrow, so that he felt uncomfortable and somehow afraid. She put her hands to a silver locket on a chain round her throat. "How can I leave Marvin?"

Sparrow had never known his parents, so he told himself he wasn't in a position to offer advice; not at the time, anyway.

"No, I see it would be difficult," he said. "Him being your dad, your lawful dad anyway. And you being a successful star and all that. And anyway, you're American, ain't you?"

But Mary was staring past Sparrow now. He looked behind him quickly and saw the tall figure of the hypnotist.

"None of those reasons keep me with Marvin," replied the girl in a dead sort of whisper. "You don't understand the power of a man like him—how could you? But he is evil!"

And, as she spoke, Marvin beckoned.

Like a well-trained animal, Mary silently went towards the tall, sinister figure, then they disappeared into their dressing-room.

"Now what was all that about?" whispered Sparrow.

He remained where he was in the shadows for a few moments, then he walked softly along the corridor.

Their dressing-room door was open slightly, showing a chink of light and allowing Sparrow a view of Marvin and the girl. It was Marvin's voice, though, that caught his attention.

"You will keep it safe," Sparrow heard, and Marvin's strange, deep, vibrant voice made him shiver. "Always safe—and secret!"

Sparrow's natural inquisitiveness was reinforced by his concern for the girl, so it was inevitable that he remained to watch and listen. Marvin's voice was strange enough, but his actions were stranger.

He was facing Mary, who was seated with her back to Sparrow, but Sparrow could see her face in the big dressing-room mirror. In his hand, Marvin held Mary's silver locket by the chain.

It swung before her in a glittering arc, backwards and forwards. "Remember!" came that weird, deep voice. "Remember, Mary—

you will stay with me and keep our secret. Do you understand, Mary?" Sparrow could not have entered the dressing-room, not, as he told Wiggins and the others later, for a handful of gold.

And when he heard Mary speak in a strange, unnatural voice, he wished himself outside in the chilly, rain-soaked streets— anywhere rather than in the music-hall. For Mary looked as if she were possessed by demons.

"I obey you," she said. "The secret is safe!"

Then, in a moment, Marvin smiled a tight-lipped smile and snapped his fingers.

"Wake, Mary!"

The girl jolted forward and put her hands to her head.

"It's almost time for the act," Marvin said. "You've been asleep, Mary—now, snap out of it, you little idiot, and put some makeup on. We don't want people thinking you're some kind of dummy, do we! Hurry it up, kid! Here, put your Ma's locket back on!"

"Yes," she murmured. "Mother's locket," she said, tears in her eyes.

"Ah, The Magical Marvin!" cried Mr. Trump as the hypnotist appeared with Mary. Sparrow jumped back from the doorway instantly.

"Just giving Mr. Marvin a call, sir!" he cried, and Mr. Trump nodded to him.

"Good, good—don't forget what I told you, Marvin," he went on to the hypnotist. "You could be playing before the Prince of Wales himself soon!"

"I'm not too sure about that," muttered Marvin.

"But you have a wonderful career ahead of you!" Mr. Trump enthused. "And you too, my dear," he told Mary.

"Chin up, I'll think of something," hissed Sparrow as Marv went past him.

But Mary stared in front of her like a sleepwalker, and it was obvious that she had not heard him.

From the auditorium, Sparrow heard the loud applause as Marvin began his mystifying act.

"Ladies and gentlemen!" called Marvin, in his deep, vibrant voice. "I have made the study of Mentalism my life's work, and tonight I shall show you the amazing powers of Hypnotism!"

There was a roll of drums and the crash of a cymbal, and Sparrow snorted loudly, for Marvin was passing his hands before the painted face and staring eyes of Mary, his stepdaughter.

"I shall show you," declared Marvin, "when I have put Mary here into a deep trance and blindfolded her, how I can communicate with her by the transfer of thoughts—by mind-reading!"

Sparrow watched as Mary apparently became drowsy.

"Now for the blindfold!" Marvin cried. "And, if you are ready, ladies and gentlemen, I will ask you to find some object you carry about your person for Mary to identify!"

Mary appeared to be in a deep trance, though she was smiling straight back at Marvin.

"Mary, are you asleep?" called Marvin, and in a slow, deep tone quite unlike Mary's normal voice she answered:

"I am asleep, Master!"

"Oh no, you're not!" muttered Sparrow from the wings where he was watching the act. "You were in a trance in the dressing-room, but you ain't in one now!"

But the audience was impressed. There was a deep, sighing sound, and in the silence Marvin's voice rang out:

"Who will be the first, if you please? Who will ask Mary to identify an object—which she cannot see!"

Someone stirred. Then another, and another. Marvin pointed at a man who held up a watch:

"You, sir! I can see what you are holding, but Mary cannot. Mary!"

"Yes, Master?"

"Tell me what the gentleman is holding in his hand! Concentrate, Mary.... Take your time. Are you ready?"

"I am ready, Master!" Mary said, putting her hands to her temples.

"Then what is it?"

"It's a—a watch!"

The audience gasped, then they clapped and finally they cheered. Mary identified a wallet correctly; and a ladies' purse; a handkerchief; and a gold ring. She was right every time.

"I reckon," whispered Sparrow to himself as the curtains closed, "that I know how you work it, Marvin—and it ain't Hypnotism or Mentalism, it's just plain faking!"

Gorgeous Gussie brushed past Sparrow.

"Get my placards up, duckie!" she called. "Why are you staring at her?"

Sparrow jumped to fetch the placards. "She's in trouble, that girl is," he told the singer. "I just wish I could do something to help her."

"How sweet of you, duckie!" cried Gorgeous Gussie. "Whoops—there's my cue, I'm on!"

She tripped on to the stage and left Sparrow still looking down the corridor which led to the artistes' dressing-rooms.

"I will do something to help Mary!" he promised himself. "But I'm all at sixes and sevens over this business. Maybe Wiggins will know what to do!"

CHAPTER TWO

But later that night over hot peas and faggots in the cellar of the derelict house which was the home of the Baker Street Boys, Wiggins for once had little to say.

Normally he would have been excited by the thought of a fresh puzzle. When he got the smell of a mystery, he would look up at the picture of Mr. Sherlock Holmes and say something like, "Now, what would he do?" or better still, "We have our methods, Mr. Holmes and me, so we do!"

All he said, however, when Sparrow had finished telling him of Mary's hatred and fear of her stepfather was:

"It ain't much to go on, is it, Sparrow?"

"What!" cried Sparrow, swallowing rapidly and burning his throat in the process. "She's in mortal terror of her life!"

"Blimey!" shivered Rosie, who was the youngest of them all. "Who'd want a stepfather what does that to you?"

"Not me!" said Queenie. "And if Mr. Holmes was here, he'd soon do something about it!"

"Yeh!" Beaver cried. "Mr. Holmes always helps those what's in danger, especially young ones and females. Sparrow ain't stupid, and if he says the girl's in mortal fear, then she is! And we've got to do something—so there!"

The rest of the Baker Street Boys joined in loudly, but Wiggins stayed silent for what seemed like hours.

"What do you think, Wiggins?" said Rosie, for Wiggins was staring at the features of the Master and she sensed that he was coming to a conclusion. It took some time in coming, though.

"I dunno," said Wiggins at last. "But I can tell you one thing for certain."

"What's that?" said Sparrow.

"We've got to get Mary away from Marvin."

"Wow!" they yelled, delighted that Wiggins had finally decided to act, especially Queenie and Rosie; for there was something particularly horrifying about Mary's plight which they felt they understood better than the boys.

"But that's not all we're going to do," Wiggins went on. "Mr. Holmes and I have our methods. We like to find out what's at the bottom of the mystery, and that's what we're going to do. If Marvin's got some nasty secret, like Sparrow says he has, then we're going to find out what it is."

"Pheww!" said Sparrow. "So what we going to do, Wiggins?"

It didn't take Wiggins long to explain. There was a lot more to the Amazing Marvin than met the eye. When Sparrow said he wasn't going to try to meet Marvin in the eye because he'd seen what Marvin could do, Wiggins agreed that they should be extra cautious.

"Yeh," agreed Queenie. "This hypnotism business is dangerous, Sparrow. You watch out for yourself in case he gets his nasty eyes on you!"

"You're going to have to be very careful too, Queenie," said Wiggins.

"Me?" said Queenie.

"Yes," said Wiggins.

"Why, what's Queenie got to be careful for?—She ain't going to get Mary away from Trump's Music-hall, is she?" said Rosie.

Queenie gazed at Wiggins for a while.

"You're planning something nasty, ain't you, Arnold Wiggins?" she said, but Wiggins wouldn't tell her anymore.

All he said was:

"We have our methods, me and Mr. Holmes."

CHAPTER THREE

Sparrow was kept even busier the next evening. Everyone seemed to want him to run some errand or other. Bert made sure that he helped the stage-hands, and Mr. Trump too seemed to be checking up on him continually.

"So you like working here, boy?" Mr. Trump said, as Sparrow waved to Gorgeous Gertie who was about to begin her first song. "I see you're a friendly sort of fellow—the artistes seem to like you."

Sparrow tried not to let his glance stray to a large basket which usually held the magician's stage-effects.

"Yessir," said Sparrow, who for once was almost at a loss for words.

"And Mr. Marvin's daughter, er, Sparrow," said Mr. Trump, "I believe you talk to her sometimes."

"Yessir!"

Sparrow trembled. What was Mr. Trump getting at? Had he heard Mary telling him that she was desperate to get away from the hypnotist's evil power? But Mr. Trump merely nodded approvingly.

"I like to see a boy that tries to get on with people," he said.

"How does Mary like it here in England—does she speak much of New York?"

"Nossir!" said Sparrow. "I didn't know she come from New York."

Mr. Trump frowned and clicked his heels. "Get on with your work," he ordered, and he walked away.

Mary was already searching for him backstage.

"Sparrow!" she called, in a low, tearful voice. "I can't stand it any longer! But every time I try to run away, my head starts to swim around and I can't drag myself away from the dressing-room! And yet I must go. I know that Marvin's about to do something dreadful! He keeps yelling out for no reason at all, and he stares out of the window all the time, wherever we are...."

"Careful!" Sparrow gulped as he heard footsteps, but he glimpsed Madame Pompadour's green chiffon dress and went on:

"I gotta be quick—I know how he keeps you with him, and it's to do with your head swimming all the time."

Mary's white face looked haunted.

Unconsciously her hands wandered to the locket at her throat.

"I dream of it too," she whispered. "I hear his voice, and I see something shining in those terrible dreams."

"He does it with your locket!" snarled Sparrow. "I saw him last night—and he's not doing it anymore!"

"Who's not doing what?" called a deep voice.

"Blimey!" gasped Sparrow. "It's Marvin!"

"What are you doing here?" growled the hypnotist suspiciously. "Are you spying on me, kid?"

Sparrow protested his innocence, but it was Mary who saved him by telling Marvin that she had asked Sparrow to fetch her a drink.

"OK, OK," Marvin growled. "Just keep away from the kid, OK?"

The evening seemed to drag by on leaden feet as Sparrow waited for the right moment; and eventually it came. He waited then for the explosion which must follow.

Sparrow was in the wings on the far side of the stage from the artistes' dressing-rooms when he heard the commotion. Voices called urgently—Mr. Trump, Marvin, Bert, and a couple of stage-hands, all of them calling increasingly loudly so that they could be heard above the sound of the orchestra.

Mary had disappeared!

"Gone?" said Sparrow innocently, as Mr. Trump crossed the stage towards him. "Who's gone?"

"Sparrow! Where is that confounded girl?" cried Mr. Trump, heedless of the calls from the audience, who were expecting the curtain to rise on the hypnotist's act. "Where is she?"

Marvin spotted Sparrow too.

"Say, kid," he called, joining the manager. "You were talking to Mary—where's my daughter?"

"Search me!" said Sparrow. "I ain't seen her for a half-hour or more—not since you said I was to keep away from her."

"Damnation and blazes!" yelled Mr. Trump. "I've got a theatre full and no act! I've got to have Marvin's act!"

"And I've got a daughter that's cut loose!" yelled Marvin. The orchestra leader poked his head through the curtains.

"And there's a restless audience out here, sir," he called to Mr. Trump. "What shall I do?"

"Don't look at me," said Marvin. "No kid, no act—she knows the routines! I'll go and look around for her."

Mr. Trump looked around wildly.

"Fetch Gorgeous Gertie back!" he called. "She'll have to do another turn—tell her it'll be another five guineas!" Then he turned to Sparrow. "Now, boy—"

But Sparrow was not there anymore.

* * * * * * *

"I can't believe it!" Mary cried when Sparrow led her into the cellar of the derelict house. "I'm free!"

Queenie and Rosie rushed to bring her to the warmth of the fire, whilst Sparrow grinned triumphantly. As for Wiggins, he simply looked smug.

"And these are your friends—all orphans, like me?" said Mary, gazing around her curiously. "I'm so grateful to you all!"

"It was Wiggins' idea to use the magician's chest to hide you," said Sparrow. "And it worked a treat, didn't it, Mary?"

"Oh, I heard Mr. Trump yelling at them to look everywhere,

and when they banged on the basket—" began Mary.

"—and looked inside—" went on Sparrow.

"—and got fooled though I was in there all the time—" gasped Mary, who managed to laugh now at the memory of her ordeal.

"—and then we waited till everyone rushed outside, and here we are," finished Sparrow, looking fondly around the cellar. "Home, sweet home."

"And I'm never going back," said Mary. "Never!"

"'Course you're not," agreed Wiggins. "Mind you, Marvin's not going to give up the act, is he? Not when there's royalty coming to see him. He's going to keep on looking for you, Mary, but when he doesn't find you, he's going to want a new girl for the act."

Mary shuddered.

"I wouldn't wish that on any poor girl!" she said.

"Yeh!" shivered Rosie. "What girl'd be fool enough to go on stage with Marvin?"

Wiggins looked from Mary to Rosie; and then to Queenie.

"But we've got to get to the bottom of this mystery," he said. "Ain't we—even if it does mean one of us working with Marvin?"

Queenie let out a long gasp.

"One of us?" she cried. "Working with Marvin—Arnold Wiggins, if you're thinking what I think you're thinking—"

"Queenie, this is our most important case!" declared Wiggins. "What's a bit of danger for the Baker Street Boys? You wouldn't mind being a star of the music-hall for a night or two would you?"

"Yes!" cried Queenie. "I won't do it! You can't make me— anyway, I can't do this Mentalism business—and I won't be put in trances!"

"Don't let that worry you," said Mary. "Marvin doesn't put me in a trance on stage. It's all a fake."

"I thought it was!" said Sparrow.

"So you could teach Queenie here the routine?" asked

Wiggins.

"In five minutes," said Mary. "But don't let her do it! It's too dangerous!"

By now, though, Queenie was won over to the idea. She was an independent-minded girl with a strong character; and she had lived by her wits all her fifteen years.

"Wiggins is right," she said briskly. "I'll be able to find out what your stepfather's really up to once I'm his new assistant. Now, what about this here routine?"

It was easier than any of them—except Sparrow—could have imagined. There was no hypnotism, and no trance—nor could Mary peep through a concealed hole in the blindfold.

It was all done by means of code-words. Mary explained it all.

Marvin would blindfold her after he pretended to hypnotise her. Then he would call on members of the audience to hold up some object. There wasn't much variation in the objects they produced. It would be a watch, say, or a wallet, or a handker-chief, or a ring—and Marvin had a code for each item.

If it was a watch, he'd say to Mary, "Now, Mary, think hard—take your time...."

"So 'Time' was the code-word for a watch," said Mary. "It's as easy as that."

"Elementary, my dear Mary, as Mr. Holmes would say," agreed Wiggins. Mary smiled at him.

"Of course it is," she agreed. "For a ring, Marvin would say, "Concentrate, Mary, don't let your thoughts wander around...."

"'Around'!" said Sparrow, as Beaver frowned. "Get it—'around'. Round! A ring's round, ain't it?"

Queenie soon picked up the routine, and it was decided that Sparrow should introduce her to Marvin the next day at the music-hall. It could hardly have gone better, though at first Marvin had his doubts.

"That brat of mine never makes a mistake," he told Sparrow and Queenie when he had got used to the idea of using her as a substitute for Mary. "You say this kid's worked in the music-halls before?"

"You try her out, Mr. Marvin, sir," said Sparrow. "She knows all the tricks, don't you, Queenie?—here, put the blindfold on."

"OK, OK," said Marvin. "We've got the cops looking for Mary, but so far she's not shown up—I got to have an act for tonight, so let's try something. You ready?"

"I'm ready," said Queenie:

"I'm holding up an object," said the hypnotist, holding up a silver cigarette case. "Come on now...concentrate hard... Queenie...."

"I know!" cried Queenie. "It's a silver case—a silver cigarette case!" Marvin relaxed.

"I guess that's one problem solved," he said, but he looked a desperately worried man. "OK, Queenie, we'll go through the whole routine, and if you know it, we'll play the show tonight. This is one performance I can't miss—not when there could be royalty coming!"

Sparrow bumped into Mr. Trump as he left Marvin's dressing-room. "Well, boy," he said anxiously. "How did it go?"

"Smashing, sir!" Sparrow told him. "Queenie's on tonight."

"And no news of poor Mary?"

"The bobbies haven't found a trace of her, Mr. Trump," Sparrow said, and as Mr. Trump turned away he muttered, "and they're not going to!"

Sparrow was kept busy until it was time for Marvin's performance; and when he next saw Queenie, he could scarcely recognise her. She wore one of Mary's red dresses, and her face was covered in stage makeup.

"Blimey," said Sparrow as she and Marvin passed him backstage. "What do you look like?"

"Like a professional performer, Sparrow," said Queenie, as the music struck up. "Now, shut up and let me concentrate—wish me luck!"

Queenie hardly faltered.

She identified watches, rings, wallets, and handkerchiefs; and her lively manner went down well with the audience. Sparrow

was delighted for her, but he was watchful. Wiggins had emphasised that they were involved in a mysterious case, and that he
and Queenie should be ready for any developments. But nothing
out of the ordinary had happened so far.

"Now, who will be the next to try the amazing powers of
Mentalism?" boomed out Marvin's deep voice. "You sir? You
wish to request this blindfolded girl to identify something—
will you pass it up?"

Sparrow craned forward.

"Is it a watch again?" hissed Madame Pompadour, who was
watching the act with him.

"No," said Sparrow. "I can't see—bit of paper, I think."

"Ah!" said Marvin, taking the paper.

And then he seemed to stagger as he looked at the object.

"What's the matter with him?" said Madame Pompadour.
"He's gone as white as a sheet!"

The audience noticed Marvin's discomposure too: and the
musicians craned forward to watch him. Seconds passed.

"I am ready, Master," said Queenie, who also realised that
the silence had gone on too long.

"Yes!" whispered Marvin, who recovered himself quickly. "It
was a note—nothing to do with the act," he said, raising his
voice. "I'm sorry for this delay, ladies and gentlemen—another
object, if you please? Yes—you, sir. Fine!"

"Now what was all that about?" said Madame Pompadour.

"Search me," said Sparrow.

"Was it that note?" she said.

"I dunno,'" he answered. "But it didn't do him any good, did
it?"

Queenie knew that there had been a disturbance of some kind
during the act, but she had no way of knowing how affected
Marvin had been. "How did I do?" she whispered as the act
came to an end amidst the applause and cheers of the audience.
"Did I do something wrong?"

"No, kid," said Marvin, hustling her towards the dressing-
room. "You did fine—now, keep out of my way!"

He was so nervous and agitated that she became alarmed and edged towards the door. All Mary's warnings came back to her; but Marvin paid her no attention. He rushed about throwing clothes into a suitcase, and looking out of the window every few seconds. And then he noticed Queenie at the door.

"Don't open that door!" he yelled.

Queenie panicked and yanked at the handle, but Marvin had her by the neck and flung her across the room before she could escape. He bolted the door and turned to her.

"Don't move, kid—OK?" he snarled. "I gotta get out of here, fast!" He dashed to the window and used his strength against the frame, but the window wouldn't budge.

And then a crash came at the door.

"Help!" screamed Queenie as she realised that Marvin was terrified of someone—someone who was breaking down the door!

Marvin turned as the door burst free and a huge brutish form rushed in. Even in her terror, Queenie heard the loud blast of music from the stage that heralded Madame Pompadour's act—no one would hear the commotion, she realised. But nevertheless she screamed again.

A blow sent her reeling, and she knew little of what followed. She was aware of a struggle; of a desperate scrabbling sound; and then she felt herself seized roughly and raised. After that, a damp cloth blocked her breathing, and the last thing she could identify was a sickly, sweet smell—and that was all, for a long time.

CHAPTER FOUR

I, Sergeant Hopkins, was in an excellent position to follow the exploits of the Baker Street Boys during the progress of the Case of the Captive Clairvoyant; for I was called to Trump's Music-hall to assist my boss, Inspector Lestrade, in a murder investigation.

Murder? Yes! Marvin lay on the floor of his dressing-room with a knife in his back, and as for Queenie, she had completely disappeared!

"I never did hold with this hypnotism business," Inspector Lestrade murmured to me as we inspected the corpse.

"It didn't do Mr. Marvin much good either, sir," said one of the many onlookers who had crowded into the room.

"What!" said the Inspector. "Who's that boy?"

I recognised him as Sparrow, one of the Baker Street Boys, but I merely said:

"One of the theatre's staff, sir—the buttons, I believe they're called."

"Don't trouble me with that now, Hopkins," the Inspector told me.

"Clear these people out and we can get on with our investigation. Get statements from them all, will you?"

"That's Signor Maccarelli's knife in him!" called out one of the artistes, a large, stout lady.

"Is someone accusing me?" cried an Italian.

"Mr. Marvin wasn't liked," put in Mr. Trump. "He was a nasty piece of work."

"It's my knife, yes!" Signor Maccarelli called above the hubbub. "But I kill nobody, ever!"

"Hopkins, get them out!" Inspector Lestrade called to me. "And I want you all to know," he said as the artistes were driven out, "that I believe I shall be able to solve this mystery only when the police are able to find the whereabouts of Mary Ashley, Marvin's missing assistant!"

Wiggins was in the corridor with Sparrow when Inspector Lestrade made this statement.

"But Mary's not involved in this here murder!" gasped Sparrow.

"Shut up!" hissed Wiggins. "Listen!"

"Yes!" Lestrade finished. "I think that young lady's deeply involved! In fact, I intend to have a warrant issued for her arrest!"

"On what charge, sir?" I asked him.

"Murder—accomplice to murder, Hopkins! I suspect that young lady of being in league with whoever murdered her step-father! From what I've heard, she had no reason to love him—and the man's dead!"

Sparrow couldn't restrain himself. He rushed forward to the Inspector:

"And what about Queenie—she's gone! She's been taken away and maybe murdered too—the window's open! That's how she was got out!"

Inspector Lestrade took a closer look.

"Now I recognise you!" he cried. "You're one of Sherlock Holmes's amateur detectives—and if I'm not much mistaken, Hopkins, there's another one down the corridor—why, it's Wiggins!"

"So it is, sir," I said to my boss.

"I will not have amateur sleuths about me!" cried Inspector Lestrade. Then another thought struck him. "Hopkins—that girl, Queenie. Don't tell me she's also one of that gang of raga-muffins?"

"I'm afraid so, sir. Do you think she has been seized? She

could be in danger, Inspector."

"Not her!" said Lestrade. "No doubt she's run off in all this commotion. And that's just what these other ragamuffins can do. Get them out, or I'll have them put in the cells for obstructing the course of this investigation!"

Wiggins and Sparrow were soon evicted by a burly constable; and when they stood in the rain-swept street, Sparrow said dejectedly:

"It wasn't such a good idea, was it, Wiggins? The bobbies will be hunting for Mary, and Lestrade's warned us off—there ain't much we can do, is there?"

Wiggins drew Sparrow under the light of a gas-lamp. He pulled a piece of paper from his pocket and showed it to Sparrow.

"That's the paper Marvin had on stage!" said Sparrow. "Where did you get it?"

"Picked it up in the dressing-room as we was ordered out," said Wiggins. "You told me what happened on stage when Marvin turned white, and I just saw it lying there when Lestrade gave us the push."

"Not much on it, is there?" said Sparrow.

"Enough," said Wiggins.

"Just one spot—what is it, rust?"

"Blood."

"Blood!" gasped Sparrow. "What's it for, then?"

"I've heard about it," said Wiggins. "It's the final warning from gangsters and such-like—it's the death-spot from a gang."

Sparrow passed the slip of paper back. "So Marvin saw it and tried to run!"

"Yeh," said Wiggins. "But he wasn't quick enough."

"Nor was Queenie," said Sparrow. "We've got to find her!"

"If she's alive," said Wiggins.

CHAPTER FIVE

Queenie awoke to find herself tied hand and foot, and with a gag in her mouth. She tried to roll over and discovered that she was lying on some kind of couch; there was a little light from the door, and when her eyes got accustomed to the gloom, she discovered that she was in a small box-room.

It was musty and cold, and she had never felt so alone or afraid. This was worse in a way than the sudden shock of Marvin's violence, and then the brutal blow from the burly thug who had hit her and then chloroformed her—for she recognised now how she had been silenced.

Thoughts tumbled endlessly through her mind. She struggled against the cords at her feet and wrists, but they would not give a fraction of an inch; she was trying to chew through the gag when a rough voice came to her from the next room.

"Hello, sir. You all right?"

"Of course! What about the girl?"

Queenie concentrated: there was something about the voice that was familiar; but it was muffled by the door and it was very faint too; the other speaker stood much nearer to her.

"The girl?" the rough voice said. "Sleeping still—tied hand and foot and gagged. Will you take a look, sir?"

"And have her able to identify me? Certainly not! Now, get back and find what I told you to find!"

"I can't go back there!" cried the rough voice. "—It's full of bobbies!"

"It will be locked by now, and the theatre's deserted—do as

I say!" the second speaker snarled, and there was the sound of a heavy blow. "Marvin had it with him! Find it!"

"All right! All right—I'm going! But what about the girl in there?" cried the thuggish voice.

Queenie had been following the conversation in an almost trance-like state. She knew she was being held captive by desperate men; but why and where was beyond her—except that it must be to do with Marvin, for both speakers knew him. It was also clear to her that the man with the rough voice was the thug who had knocked her down, and that the second speaker was his employer.

But what did they want from Marvin's dressing-room? In the midst of her fears, Queenie had one consolation: Wiggins was right again. What better way of discovering Marvin's secret could there be than to become his assistant?

Queenie froze again though when the next words came to her: "How about her?" grunted the thug before he left.

There was a pause, and Queenie heard a strange metallic sound. She couldn't identify it, but she had heard it before. It went on for several seconds, terrified, she held her breath; for she knew her fate was about to be decided. "How about her?" the thug had said. He meant, "Do we let her live?"—Queenie was sure of it.

"Let her sleep," said the second man eventually. "We can see to her later."

Queenie's breath came out in a long, deep sigh behind the gag. She heard the slam of a door and two sets of heavy foot-steps.

"See to me?" she whispered to herself. "I can see to myself!" And she started to test the knots.

* * * * * *

Wiggins had just finished telling the other Baker Street Boys about the blood-spot, when the door burst open, and a tall, thin man stood framed in the doorway. He was poorly-dressed, and yet for all his sudden and frightening entry, he didn't seem particularly threatening.

Wiggins grabbed a poker. Mary let out a scream; Rosie grabbed her. Beaver put his big fists up. And Sparrow stood behind Wiggins with a chunk of wood in his hands—whilst Shiner stood behind him.

"What'd you want!" yelled Wiggins.

"It's OK, folks!" the stranger called, a smile on his face. "No cause for alarm!"

"He's an American!" said Sparrow. "Like Mary!"

"And I've seen him before!" said Wiggins. "Who are you? You was near Trump's Music-hall earlier—have you done anything to Queenie? 'Cos if you have—"

"Here, hold it!" the stranger cried. "I'm on your side, kids, especially now I've found Miss Mary Ashley here! Cards on the table, OK—I'm O'Neill, Special Investigator for Pinkerton's Detective Agency. See, here's my card!"

"You look, Wiggins," said Sparrow, so Wiggins cautiously approached O'Neill.

"It looks genuine," he said.

"It sure is—and I happen to know about you kids working for Mr. Sherlock Holmes, so maybe you can trust me to come in and talk?" Wiggins still hesitated. He turned to Mary.

"Mary," he said. "What do you think? Do we listen to him?" O'Neill shrugged.

"It's listen to me, or listen to Inspector Lestrade. It won't be long before he works out where Mary's got to! I asked around earlier tonight, and I learned how close she'd got to Sparrow here—yes, I recognised you, Sparrow!" he said as Sparrow looked at him in amazement. "I've been in the game a long time and I know how to find out what I want to know! And however dumb Lestrade is, that young Sergeant Hopkins will soon put two and two together and come looking around here! Now, what's it to be, kids?"

"We'll listen to you, Mr. O'Neill," said Mary. "I don't think you mean us any harm."

So the Pinkerton investigator began to tell them an amazing story. "First of all, kids," he said, "I've been on the lookout for Mary Ashley's stepfather for over a year—long before he met her mother and turned himself into Marvin the Mentalist."

"Why, what's he done?" said Sparrow. O'Neill smiled.

"More than you'd believe. Marvin was a member of the worst gang of desperadoes that New York ever saw—and Marvin was one of the worst before he left the Iron Fist gang!"

"He left the gang?" said Wiggins.

"Yeah!" said the American. "With the loot—and nobody robs the Iron Fist gang and gets away with it! They've been on the lookout for him ever since!'"

"He knew they were coming!" said Mary. "He was scared— I'm sure he was!"

"He had every reason to be terrified," said O'Neill. "He made off with the loot—over a couple of million dollars worth of jewels. He knew that when they caught up with him, his life wouldn't be worth a bent nickel."

"Yet you found him, Mr. O'Neill," said Mary. "Wasn't it your duty to arrest him right away?"

"No," said O'Neill. "I've been hired to get the jewels back. We want to see the rest of the gang behind bars, but most of all the Pinkerton Agency wants the loot—and I'm not quitting yet!"

The Baker Street Boys listened in utter fascination as O'Neill told of his investigations. He had found Marvin's trail in New York only a few weeks before his appearance at the music-hall. And when finally O'Neill crossed the Atlantic to check up on one slender lead, he realised that he had found the treacherous member of the Iron Fist gang.

It had been an almost unbelievable discovery, for who would have thought that the most wanted criminal in the United States would have the nerve to appear in public on the stage? But, so O'Neill explained, when Marvin had met and married Mary's mother, he had looked quite different from The Amazing Marvin the Mentalist.

He had been heavier then, and he wore a beard and a heavy

moustache. Now, much lighter and clean-shaven, he had shown the bravado that had made him such a desperate and successful criminal.

"He sure had gall," said O'Neill. "But he fooled the gang—none of them picked up his trail."

"But surely they did!" put in Mary.

"Yeah!" said Wiggins. "And they killed him!"

O'Neill shook his head.

"I've been on the lookout for the past week," he said. "If any of the gang had been around, I'd have spotted them. That's what I've been waiting for—some of them to show up and get Marvin scared so he would panic. But someone else got to him first."

Wiggins breathed out slowly.

"'S'trewth!" he said. "If the gang didn't get him—then who did? And where's the loot?"

"I've got a clue," said O'Neill. "I have proof that Mary's step-father placed his stolen loot in a safety-deposit box in a New York bank. We don't know which bank, but we know that some-where amongst Marvin's possessions there must be a ticket of some kind that gives him access to his loot. If we can find the secret of the ticket, I can recover the jewels!"

"Marvin's secret," whispered Sparrow. "That's what it was."

Wiggins and the others looked at Sparrow in amazement, for he was staring at Mary as though she was a ghost.

"What's the trouble, kid?" asked O'Neill.

"Sparrow, tell me!" gasped Mary.

"Come on!" growled Wiggins.

"All right—I will!" cried Sparrow. "Mary's got the secret of the loot—that's why he was hypnotising her! I saw him do it with her locket—he put her in a trance and said she was never to tell his secret!"

And then Sparrow reached out to touch the silver locket at Mary's neck.

"What is it, Sparrow?" whispered Mary.

"The locket?" said O'Neill.

Wiggins nodded slowly.

"It has to be, doesn't it—let's have a look in that locket of yours, Mary."

And it was there.

Mary wept when she saw the picture of her dead mother; but when she saw that Marvin had hidden the safety-deposit box ticket behind the picture, she became furious.

"He used me just as he used my poor mother!" she cried. "He could have had me killed too!"

"Marvin sure was smart," agreed O'Neill. "When he figured the gang was after him, he made sure they couldn't get to the loot."

"He knew I'd take care of the locket!" Mary sobbed. "It's the only one of my mother's possessions he let me keep!"

Wiggins looked at the ticket for which Marvin had been killed. For a few moments he stood deep in thought, and then suddenly he looked up at the picture on the wall, at the stern features of Mr. Sherlock Holmes.

The Baker Street Boys noticed his abstraction; and so did O'Neill. "Something bothering you, kid?" he said.

"Oh yes," said Wiggins. "Quite a few things, as a matter of fact. Things like who gave the blood-spot to Marvin, for a start, and where Queenie is for another. Then again, we've got to think about this here ticket and how to catch a murderer, ain't we?"

"Yeh!" said Sparrow. "What you thinking, Wiggins?" Wiggins pointed to the picture of Mr. Holmes.

"I was thinking of what Mr. Holmes would do."

"And what's that?" said Rosie.

"Yeah, kid," said O'Neill. "This case isn't finished yet—we want Queenie back, and the way to do that is to find the murderer. You got a plan, kid?"

"Sort of," said Wiggins. "I'm going to see Dr. Watson to ask him to send a telegram to Mr. Holmes, but meanwhile we'll need Inspector Lestrade's help."

"Lestrade!" said Sparrow. "But he won't have us near him!"

"He will when we take Mary to him," said Wiggins.

"You're not taking Mary!" cried Rose. "He thinks she helped the murderer!"

"True," said Wiggins. "But Mr. O'Neill and me might persuade him different."

"How?" said O'Neill. Wiggins looked smug.

"I don't know much about America," he told O'Neill, "but I did hear how they catch wolves out there."

"Wolves, kid?"

"Yeh," said Wiggins. "They put out wolf-bait."

He showed O'Neill and the fascinated Baker Street Boys the ticket. Then he slipped it back into the locket and fastened the locket around Mary's neck.

"What are you doing that for?" whispered Mary.

O'Neill understood:

"Wolf-bait!"

* * * * * *

Queenie struggled for hours in the dingy box-room; at one time, she thought the cords at her wrists had given a little, but before she could be sure, exhaustion overtook her.

As the cold grey light of another dawn filtered into the box-room, Queenie slept.

Her dreams were full of terror.

CHAPTER SIX

"What!" cried Inspector Lestrade to me when he first heard early the next morning that the Baker Street Boys were again involved.

"Amateurs again? I won't have it, Hopkins! No ragamuffin amateurs are going to impede this investigation! It's bad enough having a wretched American investigator up to his neck in gangsters and stolen jewels poking about here, but I will not have those would-be sleuths near me! Get a statement from each of them, Hopkins, and see if you can find something to charge them with."

I told my superior that it wasn't likely that I could.

"Charge them with abducting the girl—what's her name?"

"Mary Ashley, sir. But they didn't abduct her, from what I understand of the situation. Wiggins—"

"Don't speak to me, about Wiggins! Mr. Holmes might hold him in high regard, but so far as I'm concerned he's just another meddling urchin!"

It had seemed an easy business at first. There was the dead gangster (as we found him to be once O'Neill reported to us) stretched out on his dressing-room floor with a knife through his heart; but Maccarelli the knife-thrower could prove that he had been drinking in company at the time of the murder.

One by one, everyone who had access to the backstage area produced an alibi of sorts. Not every alibi was perfect—a dozen different people could have slipped into the star's dressing-room and knifed him in a moment. But who had actually done it?

"One of these desperadoes," said Inspector Lestrade. "O'Neill told us they're a murderous bunch wanting their revenge on Marvin."

But O'Neill had also told us that he didn't believe the Iron Fist gang had located Marvin. So we were thrown back again into looking for the murderer amongst the music-hall people, and worse still, from Lestrade's point of view, we were forced to listen to a gang of amateurs who claimed to be able to solve the case!

"Oh, send them in!" declared my boss. "I've listened to O'Neill, so I might as well hear what Wiggins has got to say."

I did point out that, but for Sparrow's resourcefulness, Mary Ashley might also be dead, with a knife-thrust through her heart; but Inspector Lestrade snorted angrily:

"This isn't an investigation, it's chaos!"

And when he heard the American and the Baker Street Boys outlining their plan he gasped:

"It isn't chaos—it's lunacy! What, wolf-bait? Wolf-bait! And you, Miss Ashley, have agreed to be the bait?—Why, it's plain lunacy!"

It was not as lunatic a proposal as it seemed, and eventually Inspector Lestrade agreed to it.

Wolf-bait was as good a way of describing Wiggins' scheme as any—but Mary Ashley was the bait, and the unknown knife-wielder was our quarry.

It was an audacious scheme. Quite simply, we were going to put Mary back on the stage on the music-hall. She would take part in the act she knew so well, and we hoped that the murderer would make an attempt to find the secret he had already killed once for.

"It sure is a crafty kind of plan," said O'Neill in the stunned silence that followed Wiggins' and Sparrow's explanations.

"Crafty isn't what I'd call it," said Inspector Lestrade sourly. "And who's to be the new Marvin, always supposing I agree to this imbecile scheme?"

Wiggins grinned.

"In a posh suit—me!"

"Wiggins knows the act, Inspector," said Sparrow. "And there'd be crowds wanting to see Mary now her old man's been knifed—it'll be sensational!"

"And it will bring the murderer out of hiding, Inspector," said O'Neill. "We'll let it be known that Marv has inherited something of great value. It's bound to attract the murderer."

"'Course!" declared Sparrow. "It's as plain as the nose on your face!" which was an unfortunate thing to say, for Inspector Lestrade's nose was large and red.

Inspector Lestrade glared back at Sparrow; but the more he heard, the more he was convinced, and so it was that the following day's newspapers were full of the revival of Marvin's popular act—minus the murdered Marvin, but with a mysterious hypnotist called Arnold Wiggins.

And, of course, Mary Ashley!

* * * * * * *

People flocked to the opening night.

What made it more attractive for them was the promise that all the acts which had performed on the night of the murder of Marvin would again be assembled. Crowds clamoured to get into Trump's Music-hall, for what greater thrill could there be than to see the orphaned Mary in the music-hall where there had been such a gruesome murder?

"Full house!" said Mr. Trump to Bert. "Excellent!"

"Sparrow!" called Bert. "Placards for Signor Macaroni!"

"Maccarelli!" yelled the knife-thrower. "Don't make bad jokes about me, or maybe I stick a knife in you, Bert!"

"Did you hear that, Hopkins?" demanded Lestrade, who was with me backstage. "A threat!"

"Macaroni wouldn't harm a fly!" said Sparrow.

"Hush!" said Rosie. "Keep a good look out!"

"Quite," said Lestrade, so we settled back in our dusty hiding-place amongst rolls of painted canvas and miscellaneous stage-furniture whilst knives were thrown, the songs were sung, and the rest of the show was performed until, at last, with a roll of drums and a crash of cymbals, Arnold Wiggins, The Boy Hypnotist in a borrowed suit, and Mary Ashley appeared.

How the audience loved it!

They gasped and cheered, they clapped and stamped their feet, they shouted and struggled to become one of those chosen to take the stage and have a ring, or a watch, or a wallet identified. Wiggins turned out to be a most competent stand-in, too.

He hadn't had the training or the stage presence of Marvin, of course; but his confident bearing dominated the audience, and his loud voice made him a passable stage hypnotist.

I was quite enjoying the show, but Lestrade had become very impatient.

"Wolf-bait!" he growled. "Hypnotism! Amateur sleuths!" But the amateur was doing very well on stage.

"Now Mary!" he called. "You can't see a blooming thing can you?"

"No, Master!" said Mary.

"And you don't know what's in my hand, do you? She don't," he told the audience. "Not yet, 'cos she can't read my mind yet!"

The audience yelled for him to read Mary's mind, so Wiggins grinned and went on:

"Concentrate, Mary, my dear! Wipe your mind clear and concentrate! Are you ready?"

"Yes, Master...I see...I believe it is a handkerchief!"

Howls of approval greeted Mary's words. The audience cheered on and demanded more, and it was an exhausted—but exhilarated—Wiggins and Mary that finally left the stage.

"And still no sign of the murderer!" growled Lestrade.

"He's not shown his hand yet, sir," I answered. "But he couldn't tackle Mary on stage, could he? Oh, by the way, sir, I've just heard that we have two distinguished visitors in the audience!"

"Not the Prince of Wales!" gasped Lestrade. "Trump told me that he's been expecting royalty to see the act!"

"No, sir. It's Mr. Sherlock Holmes and Dr. Watson—they're

in a box at the back of the hall."

"As if I didn't have enough amateurs backstage!" Lestrade muttered. "We've got to do something to make that murderer reveal himself! But how!"

* * * * * * *

We were completely at a loss.

We had no way of knowing that poor brave Queenie was just struggling free of her bonds; nor that one of those unexpected turns of fortune which are the downfall of so many villains was even now occurring.

* * * * * * *

"I'm glad that's over!" sighed Mary, as she reached the fatal dressing-room. "And I never want to see this place after tonight."

"But we've not seen the murderer yet—or at least he ain't tried to grab you," said Wiggins. "And Queenie—where's she?"

Mary put her hand instinctively to the locket.

"Poor Queenie—I'd give all the jewels to have her back! But I don't want this locket with me anymore! I'm scared, Wiggins!"

"Scared, who's scared?" called Mr. Trump from the doorway. "Can I be of any assistance?"

Mary gave a sigh of relief

"Please put this away in your safe, Mr. Trump—I daren't go around in it any longer."

Mr. Trump took the locket.

"But of course, Mary—hello, what's that noise?"

Heavy boots pounded in the corridor, and a burly police-constable rushed by. He ignored Mr. Trump and headed for Inspector Lestrade.

"Sir—we've spotted him!" he called. "A big, nasty thug, just got in!"

"Trouble?" said Mr. Trump. "I'll put this locket away and come up front."

Wiggin's and Mary ran to find the others who were all together on the deserted stage. Everyone milled around trying to find out what was happening, and when the news spread that a thug was loose, there was panic. And then came the sound of a scream.

"Mary!" gasped Sparrow. "That's her!"

"Where?" I snapped.

"Trump's office!" Sparrow shouted back.

"She was here—a second ago!" Wiggins cried; but already he and Sparrow were pushing their way through the yelling crowd. I followed as fast as I could, but one after another of the artistes got in my way.

"Is it another murder?" cried Madame Pompadour.

"I don't know—let me loose!" I yelled back, and I could hear Inspector Lestrade trying to break free of Signor Maccarelli, who was yelling something about his knives.

"Chaos!" yelled Lestrade. "Chaos!"

I reached the office a few seconds after Wiggins and Sparrow. Mary was safe, but her attacker was dead.

He lay on the floor with a knife in his back—just like Marvin.

"There!" Wiggins said, holding the terrified girl. "It's all right, he can't harm you now!"

And he could not. He was a big, powerfully-built thug with an ugly face and the hands of a prize-fighter. In one of his hands was a silver chain—but no locket!

"Ah!" cried Lestrade. "We've got him!"

"We ain't," said Sparrow. "We've got the one that handed Marvin the note with the blood-spot. I recognise him!"

"Yes," said Wiggins. "We've got the bloke that worked for the murderer, himself—and here's Queenie!" he yelled as Queenie rushed into the room.

"Mary!" she cried.

"Oh, Queenie, you're back!" gasped Mary, and the two girls rushed into one another's arms.

But Queenie detected something that we had missed.

"Chloroform!" she cried. "He's the one that grabbed me! I can smell it!"

I opened the dead man's other hand and found a chloroform pad.

"So we've got the accomplice," said Lestrade. "But not the murderer."

O'Neill entered the office.

"And the murderer's got Mary's locket," he said. "Not that that's going to help him—we weren't foolish enough to leave the deposit-box ticket in it."

"But who is he!" growled Lestrade. "Queenie—did you see anyone, apart from this brute?"

"No! I was in the other room—I only got a glimpse of this horrible bloke, and the other one kept well out of sight," she said. "And he kept his voice down too."

"But surely you'd recognise something about him?" I said.

"Anything!" cried Wiggins. "We've got to find him Queenie, or Mary's always going to be in danger!"

Queenie. shook her head hopelessly.

"I was lying there for hours trying to identify him I can't think of anything! Except...."

"Yes!" cried Lestrade.

"Think, please, Queenie!" sobbed Mary. "I can't live with this hanging over me."

"I've got it!" cried Queenie, and she held her hand up for silence. "Listen!"

There was a slight metallic clicking sound from outside. Queenie pointed to the door.

"That's what I heard!"

"What is it?" cried Lestrade, as Sparrow flung himself through the door, followed by Wiggins, Beaver, Shiner, and myself—in that order.

"Trump!" cried Sparrow, as he darted after the owner of Trump's Music-hall. "He always clicks his heels like that!—get him!"

It all began so quickly that the police-constables were bewildered; and only the Baker Street Boys were fast enough to spot him.

Trump knew his own theatre better than anyone. He fled into the deep gloom and was lost from sight until Sparrow spotted him.

"There he goes!" he yelled. "See, he's making for that balcony—there's an exit to the roof! We'll never find him if he gets up there!" Trump leapt for a trapeze.

He turned and grinned savagely at his pursuers; he knew he had only to swing up on to the balcony to be free.

Then Wiggins spotted someone above him: "It's up to you, sir!" he yelled.

"Who's up there?" cried Lestrade. Queenie laughed.

"Mr. Holmes!"

At that moment, Mr. Sherlock Holmes leant forward and slashed the ropes; and the heavy bulk of the murderer crashed to the stage!

Dr. Watson peered down:

"Ah, Lestrade," he said. "I see you've got your man?"

"Damnation!" hissed Lestrade.

"Maybe we should offer our thanks to Mr. Holmes," I suggested. "It would be tactful, sir?"

"Yes, yes!" conceded Lestrade. "Many thanks, Mr. Holmes, sir!"

"And to Queenie?"

"If I must!"

"And the rest of the Baker Street Boys, sir?"

Lestrade forced himself to make a speech of congratulations and thanks, in which the artistes and stage-hands joined. O'Neill came forward to thank Mr. Holmes and the Boys on behalf of his clients, and also to make sure that Mary—and Queenie—were recovering from their ordeal.

Later, the American talked to them about the case—and Mary Ashley's future.

"I guess that wraps it up," he said. "Mary's going back to the States. I'm going to collect the loot. The mystery's finished and the case is solved. I had a few words with Mr. Holmes before I came here, and he said that Wiggins was right to call him in, though he's sorry he came so late. I guess you know that he's still trying to find Moriarty?"

"Of course," said Wiggins. "But Mr. Holmes came the right time, didn't he."

"Just like the Baker Street Boys," said O'Neill.

"Ah," said Wiggins. "We have our methods."

THE CASE OF THE DISAPPEARING DESPATCH CASE

CHAPTER ONE

I had been recording the exploits of the Baker Street Irregulars, which is how Mr. Sherlock Holmes referred to the gang of street urchins he occasionally employed, for only a few months when one of their most hazardous adventures took place,

I have called it "The Case of the Disappearing Despatch Case," though Sparrow suggested that a better title would be "Things ain't always what they seems." He should know, since he was present at the start of the adventure.

There is no doubt that Mr. Holmes would have taken over the case had he not been desperately ill; but he had just been seriously wounded by the evil Professor Moriarty, and the poison from Moriarty's sword-stick still ran in his veins.

He was able to help in the affair when it seemed that the bizarre mystery would never be solved, however, though as Mr. Holmes said later, the entire credit must lie with the Baker Street Irregulars for its successful outcome.

It all began one vile midwinter evening at a time when most of the shops had put up their shutters and the only people to be seen in the thick, yellow fog were either hurrying home to a fireside—or trying to earn a few pence.

Even those few had had enough of the raw, dank, chilly fog.

"Let's pack up, Rosie," Shiner called. "Look at me hands. They're dropping off. There ain't no one wanting shoeshines, not at this time of night. Let's pack up."

"Here," said Rosie, who was no bigger than Shiner. They were both small, undernourished children of about twelve years of age, wearing all the clothes they possessed. Rosie held a couple of hot chestnuts in her ragged mitt.

"What's that?" shivered Shiner.

"Hot and good," said Rosie. "Got them from the hot chestnut man up the street. One each."

"It's hot!" yelled Shiner, juggling the chestnut from hand to hand.

"What did I tell you?" said Rosie, grinning at him. "Ain't it just come off the stove?"

Shiner stopped his complaints as he heard footsteps a few yards away. He slipped the hot chestnut into his pocket and seized the tools of his trade.

"Shoeshine, sir?" he called, as a distinguished-looking elderly gentleman came into view through the swirling fog. "Do you a good one, best in London for two-pence."

The man hesitated as he saw Shiner and Rosie, and the two children saw he had a look of compassion on his face.

"Loverly flowers, sir?" said Rosie, trying to smile in spite of the freezing fog that chapped her lips and rasped in her throat. "Only tuppence a bunch, sir."

Shiner held his breath. He had been out on the streets since before dawn, and all day he had taken only sevenpence. Rosie's stock of flowers was still almost untouched, since she had not been able to afford the best and freshest blooms in Covent Garden that morning, and it was a sad-looking display of wilted flowers that she offered so hopefully to the customer.

But her smile was perfection.

"Here's threepence," said the elderly gentleman, taking the bunch she offered. "Keep the penny change for that smile of yours, my dear. I won't wait for a shoeshine," he added to Shiner, "but I'll remember your face when I come this way again, boy."

He went on his way smiling, leaving Rosie looking at the silver threepenny piece and Shiner packing up his brushes.

"I ain't got a lovely smile, Rosie," he said, "but never mind. Threepence is threepence, and that's enough for one night— Here!" he yelled as someone charged into them, sending them flying.

"My threepenny—where's it gone?" cried Rosie. "Who was that? Clumsy great bloke!"

A big figure vanished into the mist and the two children yelled until the sound of his heavy footsteps was lost in the fog. They scrabbled about searching for the silver coin which had been sent spinning from Rosie's hand. Neither of them had seen where it had fallen.

They were still peering at the ground when two more of the Baker Street Boys joined them. They were Beaver, a biggish boy of about fourteen, and Sparrow, who at eleven or so had much in common with the quick-witted town-bird he had been named after.

"What have you lost?" called Sparrow. "Dropped your diamonds, have you, Rosie?" he asked her, though Rosie ignored him.

Beaver dumped the pile of newspapers he had been carrying. "What we looking for, Rosie?" he too asked.

"A thrupenny piece," said Rosie. "A big bloke with a stick in his hand just knocked me and Shiner flying."

"I saw him," said Sparrow. "Six-foot and more, and a big red beard. He looked as though he was after something going along like the clappers, he was. He wasn't the one what gave you the thrupenny, was he?"

"Don't be daft," said Shiner. "He's the kind what'd give you a crack with his stick, that's all. Found it!" he cried.

Beaver inspected the threepenny piece.

"Got it from an old fellow," said Rosie. "He gave me the penny extra 'cos I smiled at him—he said I'd got a loverly smile. Then he walks off grinning to himself. A toff, he is."

"I saw him too," said Beaver. "Tall and thin, that him?"

"Yeh," said Sparrow. "He was carrying a little case, wasn't he? I saw him go off into a tobacconist's at the end of Baker Street— old Merriman's who buys a paper off of us."

"How about the big bloke with the stick?" said Shiner. "Where did he get to?"

"Sparrow saw him, not me," said Beaver.

"Why?" asked Sparrow, grinning at Shiner. "You going to give him a piece of your mind for knocking into you? I'd say he's big enough to put you into his pocket, and your brushes too, Shiner!"

The dispute might have gone on a little longer if Rosie hadn't stopped it by walking off into the fog saying that she had heard enough and she was hungry, and if some smartalecks wanted to stand around the street arguing, that was their lookout. But she, Rosie, was going home.

She hadn't been walking for long when the others joined her, and no sooner had they caught up with her than the incident occurred which was to set off the whole series of events of the Disappearing Despatch Case. It began with a cry from the direction of Merriman's shop.

"Oh, do help me someone!" quavered what sounded like an old woman's voice. "Help!"

"Here!" called Beaver, who was ahead of the others. "Come on!" They all ran after him, with Shiner and Rosie struggling with their belongings towards the sounds of a fierce struggle and more terrified calls for help.

"Hold on!" yelled Sparrow. "We're coming!"

Beaver and Sparrow arrived simultaneously at the source of the cries, and they were in time to see what happened. Outside Merriman's shop, a struggle was taking place.

"It's him with the red beard!" yelled Sparrow to Rosie and Shiner. The big man was struggling with an old woman who was trying to keep possession of a shopping-basket by flailing with her umbrella at him. As he grabbed at the basket, she countered with a blow at his face, but he gave a snarling cry and then he had her by one huge hand around the throat.

"Get him!" yelled Sparrow, pushing the larger boy forward.

Beaver rushed towards the man with his fists raised, but already help was on the way. From inside the well-lit tobacconist's shop, a tall figure emerged, blinking against the sudden gloom of the drifting yellow fog but quickly grasping what was happening.

In a loud and commanding voice, the elderly gentleman who had given the threepenny piece to Rosie called out:

"Why, you villain—leave her alone! Merriman, sound your whistle for the police!"

And without any further reflection, he dropped his parcels and despatch case and raised his silver-mounted cane as he approached the burly ruffian and his struggling, gasping victim.

Beaver and Sparrow were already engaged, but not for long.

"Knock his legs from under him!" yelled Sparrow to Beaver as they dodged both the umbrella and the burly man's wide, sweeping blows. "He'll have that poor old lady dead, strangled, so he will—aaaah!"

And Sparrow found himself hurled into the cobbled street as the red-bearded man snarled and caught him with a hard blow to the head. Beaver too was unable to give much assistance, for the ruffian could easily handle a terrified old woman and a couple of ragamuffins at the same time; in a moment, he had knocked Beaver too out of the fight, so that when Rosie and Shiner appeared through the gloom the first thing they saw was the two members of the Baker Street Boys struggling to their feet and wailing that they were bleeding to blinking death.

"Now, you villain, try fighting a man!" they heard the distinguished-looking elderly man call, and they saw him cut at the attacker's head with his cane.

Had the blow landed, it would have taken much of the fight out of the robber, but somehow it missed—perhaps by chance, perhaps by a fortunate glance from the poor old woman's umbrella; certainly, it was a powerful and well-aimed blow in true cavalry style. It was, however, ineffective, and worse than that it served to enrage the burly robber even more.

"Yaaargh!" he snarled, turning to face his new adversary, and Rosie quailed as she saw the beetling brows and the wild-eyed stare of the robber, whilst it took all of Shiner's resolution to begin his own attack, hacking at the man's shins.

That too was ineffectual, for before Shiner could attempt to kick the red-bearded man, the latter had dashed the stick from the elderly gentleman's hand and knocked him to the ground. Shiner saw the attacker scrabble for the cudgel at his belt to finish off the fallen old man, so he pressed home his own attack and kicked him hard on the ankle.

"Teufel!" howled the attacker, shocked by the blow. "Aaaarh!" he cursed, the cudgel now in his hand, his mad eyes promising revenge, and his whole face a mask of such rage that Shiner fled. A loud blast on a whistle stopped him.

It was the call which would summon any nearby police-officer, and the attacker clearly knew its meaning. He looked around him and saw both Beaver and Sparrow on their feet, both with a look of fierce determination on their faces. He looked further and saw that his victim was by no means completely cowed, for she still retained her umbrella in her hand.

And when he glanced towards the tobacconist's shop, he could see that Merriman had taken the opportunity of arming himself with a sturdy truncheon. The odds were too much for him, and without another moment's delay, he turned and ran into the fog, with Merriman's cries ringing after him:

"Stop that man—stop, thief!"

CHAPTER TWO

Beaver and Sparrow needed no prompting, nor did Shiner now that he was in the company of two of the bigger Baker Street Boys. Hearts pounding and lungs aching with the cold, they rushed along the alleyways after the red-bearded villain.

Rosie decided that her place was with Mr. Merriman and the victims of the robber's attack. The old woman was moaning and clutching her neck where she had been grabbed; whilst the distinguished elderly gentleman lay in a pool of blood, glistening in the flickering gaslight.

Mr. Merriman was so agitated that he was unable to decide what should be done.

"You can stop blowing that whistle," Rosie told him. "There won't be any coppers around now—they'll all be in the pub up Baker Street. Here, listen to this toff's heart—is he a goner?"

"A goner?" cried Mr. Merriman, hurrying to where Rosie bent to listen at the elderly. gentleman's chest. "I hope not, indeed I hope not! That's Sir Alfred Connyngham, one of my regulars. Is that blood?"

"'Course it's blinking blood," said Rosie, accustomed to the violence of London's streets. "And if you don't get a doctor to him soon, he'll be a goner for sure, dead as mutton, that's what."

"A doctor?" whispered Mr. Merriman. "Where am I going to find a doctor for him? And look at this poor lady too! She's fainting clean away, what with that brute's hands on her neck. Look at her! I don't know what to do!"

"You take her inside your shop, Mr. Merriman, while I see to this toff here—what did you say his name was?"

Sir Alfred Connyngham groaned just then.

"Whoever he is, he's still wiv us," Rosie went on, as Mr. Merriman dithered and moaned. "Go on—get the old girl inside. And just you keep still, your lordship or whatever you are—can you hear me?"

Again Sir Alfred groaned, and Mr. Merriman saw the sense in getting one of the victims off the street.

"You're all right," Rosie assured the elderly gentleman. "You've been bashed by a bully, but you'll live, and the old girl's all right too that you tried to help—there, old Merriman's took 'er inside, so stop worrying, will yer?"

Slowly and painfully, the old woman was half-supported into the shop, clutching her shopping-basket, her umbrella, and Merriman's arm; however, her dress was askew, and as she passed beside the half-conscious nobleman and Rosie, a handkerchief slipped from her pocket.

"Here," began Rosie, but the woman didn't hear her, so Rosie dabbed at the wound on Sir Alfred's forehead with it. "Don't want to hurt you," she told him, "but it's a nasty sight—no, don't try to sit up. You've been hit hard—and you don't deserve it, a kind old gent like you."

"Rosie?" called a familiar voice through the yellow gloom. "You there, Rosie?"

"Yeh—and you can get busy, Sparrer," called Rosie back, as first Sparrow, then Beaver, and finally Shiner puffed and panted into view.

"Lost him!" cried Shiner. "We was right up to him and he just vanished!"

"Like magic, it was," agreed Sparrow. "Beaver nearly had his coat-tails when—"

"When you lost him, and that'll do for now about him," said Rosie. "We'll see to this gentleman now he's coming round a bit—Sparrer, you hop it and fetch Dr. Watson smart now—go on!" she cried, and Sparrow ran off without argument, which was unusual for him, while Beaver and Shiner helped prop up

Sir Alfred.

"Can we get him inside?" said Beaver. "It's miserable cold out here. You ready to move, sir?" he asked the semiconscious nobleman.

"Where's Mr. Merriman, Rosie?"

"He's in too much of a dither to help," she told Beaver. "Let's get you up, sir," she said to Sir Alfred. "Beaver's right—you'll freeze out here. What's that?" she went on, hearing a faint inquiry from the injured man. "The old girl, you say?"

"Poor lady—what happened to her?" whispered Sir Alfred, who was slowly recovering his senses.

"Don't trouble yourself, Sir Alfred!" called Merriman, who reappeared from inside his shop. "I've settled her into the snug before a fire, and she's taken care of. But we must see to you, Your Lordship—here, give a hand, will you?" he said to Beaver and Shiner. "This is Sir Alfred Connyngham, you know, a member of the Government!"

"Is he now?" said Shiner, who was deeply impressed by the news.

"Easy, Your Lordship!" cried Merriman, who had managed to control his initial panicky reaction. "The police will be here before long—and a doctor! Did you send for a doctor, girl?" he asked Rosie.

"'Course I did," said Rosie. "Dr. Watson from Baker Street!"

"Ah, of course!" said Merriman. "Why didn't I think of him?" There was a groan from the injured nobleman then.

"Give a hand here!" ordered Merriman.

"Lean on me, sir," said Beaver, offering a solid shoulder to the tottering man, and slowly they walked through the dense fog towards the shop.

They were able to see the brightly-lit shop-window as a hazy beacon in the gloom, and just as the two boys and Merriman—and Rosie, adding her wiry strength—supported Sir Alfred towards the open door, a member of the London police answered Merriman's urgent summons.

"Who blew that whistle?" demanded PC Boot, clattering

towards them. "Here, what's happening—Mr. Merriman, who's these here ragamuffins?"

"Good Samaritans, all of them!" answered Merriman sharply. "You took your time, my man, for I blew I don't know how many times on my whistle—where were you, Boot? This is your beat, isn't it?"

Boot began to apologise for the delay when Merriman found another subject for his nervous anger.

This time it was a short, slim-built, middle-aged man with bushy side-whiskers and a plaid cape and hat, who was clutching a large holdall of the kind termed a carpet-bag, and, to Merriman at least, he seemed to be an intrusion on the scene, for the tobacconist said:

"I'm sorry, sir, I have not a moment to spare for you—not a single moment, sir! I can't serve you, no matter who you may be, for Sir Alfred needs my attention!"

The man turned and left and the mystery took another turn, for Sir Alfred was then reminded of his own possessions.

"Merriman!" he cried, suddenly recovering. And then he recognised the presence of a policeman too. "Constable?" he said, puzzled momentarily. "I was attacked—yes! I had my despatch case—Do you have it, Officer?"

"Me, sir? I only just arrived this instant, sir, and I'm afraid I know nothing of—"

Once more, Boot was cut short, for with a loud cry Sir Alfred Connyngham realised the extent of his loss.

"Let me go!" he cried to the two boys and to Merriman. "Who's this? Why, it's the flower-girl. Yes, you helped me, I recall it now. My things—where are they?"

"Here's your stick, sir," said Shiner. "And your tobacco parcel from the smell of it—and here's the flowers, not much to say for them, I'm afraid—"

"But my despatch case!" cried Sir Alfred. "It's black, and it has the insignia of the Crown. It must be here," he said, staggering and almost falling to the ground once more.

PC Boot might have been slow in arriving, and he certainly

had been slowwitted in allowing himself to be criticised by the tobacconist, but at the mention of official matters he immediately understood his duty.

"I believe I am addressing Sir Alfred Connyngham, am I right, Your Lordship?" he said, and he put one burly arm below the nobleman's elbow and helped him towards the shop.

"Yes," mumbled Sir Alfred. "Indeed you are, Officer," he went on as he struggled to remain conscious. "You must find my despatch case immediately! It contains important Government papers—"

He did not finish his remarks as he blacked out once more, and Boot had to take the whole of his weight.

Boot settled the nobleman into the shop, and addressed Merriman briskly, for at the mention of Sir Alfred's loss he immediately understood his duty.

"You look after His Lordship," he said to the tobacconist. "You," he told Beaver, "get yourself up the road to the police-station as if seven devils was after you—bring the Duty Officer and some men, and say Sir Alfred Connyngham's hurt—hop it! And you two," he told Rosie and Shiner, "you two help me look for this case."

Beaver ran off as he was told. The evening had begun with a fight, which in itself was exciting enough, followed by a chase that had resulted in a mystery. And now he was acting on behalf of a Government Minister—it was almost as good as being employed by Mr. Holmes himself!

Rosie and Shiner were less happy.

"It's gone," said Rosie, after she and Shiner and PC Boot had searched every inch of the area.

"It can't have," said Boot. "Are you two sure he had it with him? I mean, the poor gentleman isn't feeling quite himself just now, what with the crack he had."

But Rosie was sure that Sir Alfred had had the despatch case when he bought the flowers from her; she recalled seeing him hitch it under his arm when he reached for his pocket to pay her.

Boot looked unhappy too as they returned to Merriman's

shop. "This," he said, "will be a bad business. It has all the hallmarks—here, that's Dr. Watson in with Sir Alfred, ain't it?"

"Yeh," said Shiner. "Now if he'd got Mr. Sherlock Holmes wiv him we wouldn't be in such a tizzy. But he's not here, or he'd have it all puzzled out in half a tick."

"Maybe he would, and maybe he wouldn't," said Boot, entering the shop. "But this is a job for a professional. Now, keep back and hush. 'Evening, sir," he said to Dr. Watson.

Dr. Watson looked up and grunted as he finished inserting a stitch into a long wound on the unconscious nobleman's forehead.

"PC Boot at your service," went on the constable. "It's a nasty business. Matter of an attack on an old woman and Sir Alfred Connyngham intervening on her behalf and losing his important State documents, sir."

Dr. Watson looked up and nodded to the Baker Street Boys, who kept discreetly in the background, their eyes shining with excited interest.

"I heard from Sparrow what had happened, or part of it anyway," he said. "It was smart of him to think of me—Sir Alfred needed instant attention. Merriman told me a little too, but so far no one's mentioned an old lady. I know about a red-bearded brute who can walk through brick walls, and I know from Sir Alfred's ramblings that some extremely important documents were contained in his despatch case, but what's this about an old lady being injured? I should look at her too—good grief, Merriman, what's the matter with you?" he demanded, for the tobacconist was acting in a strange manner.

"Where is she?" the tobacconist was bleating, as he pointed to the inner room he used as a snug.

It was a small room, with one tiny window and no outside door. And it was obvious to all those who could see inside that it was quite empty.

"Where is who?" snapped Dr. Watson.

"The old girl," said Shiner.

"What was being strangled," added Rosie.

"What Merriman brought in here, sir," finished PC Boot.

"The old lady who was the subject of the red-bearded brute's attack?" said Dr. Watson.

"Yes, Doctor," said Merriman, who had recovered his wits by now. "Didn't you see her come out, sir?" Boot asked Dr. Watson.

"No, my man, I didn't. Merriman too will tell you that no one passed through his shop from the time I arrived to attend to Sir Alfred," Dr. Watson told him.

"And I'd have seen her from down the street if she'd gone while we were searching for the despatch case." said Boot.

"And us," said Shiner.

"That's another one what's disappeared," said Sparrow. "Just like magic."

"Only nastier," said Rosie.

Just then, Boot heard the clatter of a hansom arriving, followed by loud calls from a commanding voice.

PC Boot turned pale, but he tried to sound reassuring.

"I hear Inspector Lestrade calling," he said. "Excuse me, sir, I'm sure we'll have the villain arrested shortly, and the rest of this business cleared up."

With that, he left to greet Inspector Lestrade.

"Lestrade?" grunted Dr. Watson. "I fear it will take more than Inspector Lestrade's brains to puzzle out tonight's mystery."

CHAPTER THREE

"Then what happened?" said Wiggins.

Rosie and Shiner, together with Beaver and Sparrow, were wolfing down the Irish stew that Queenie had made from four-pennyworth of scrag-end of mutton and some vegetables she had picked up from the litter around the stalls at Covent Garden that morning.

Wiggins felt slightly peeved that this was his first news of the night's adventure since, at fifteen, he was the oldest of the street urchins who lived in the cellar of the derelict house near Baker Street.

He looked up at the framed picture of Sherlock Holmes and told himself that patience was one of the Master's qualities; but the effect of his warning to himself didn't last long.

"Can't you stop eating for a minute and talk?" he demanded.

"I likes my stew hot," announced Sparrow.

"Queenie's stew's too good not to eat hot!" agreed Shiner.

"I'll tell you," said Beaver, mopping his plate with a crust. "Inspector Lestrade told us to hop it and let him get on wiv the case."

"That's right," agreed Rosie. "'Hopkins,' he says to Hopkins. 'Get a statement from those ragamuffins and clear them out of my way. There's important State documents gone missing, and I can't be interrupted by a crew of would-be child-detectives.' That's what he says to Sergeant Hopkins."

Rosie had reported Lestrade's words with great faithfulness, and you may as well know how I knew. It is here that I, Sergeant

Hopkins, must reveal myself, just as Dr. Watson recorded the exploits of Mr. Holmes, so I have attempted to leave a record of those adventures and incidents in which the great man was involved only to a limited extent; I mean, of course, the activities of the Baker Street Irregulars, who, at the time I speak of were being questioned by their leader, Arnold Wiggins.

"He called us what!" demanded Wiggins of Rosie. "'Would-be detectives?'"

"That's what he said," agreed Sparrow.

"Cheek!" growled Wiggins. "Why, Mr. Holmes said to us only a few weeks back that we're more use than a dozen of the bobbies, each one of us! As for Lestrade, he wouldn't know a clue if it bit his ankle for him."

"And he said to Merriman he was glad Mr. Holmes wasn't around too," announced Beaver.

"Did he tell you that in the cab?" said Wiggins, who was practically fuming by this time.

"In the cab!" laughed Beaver. "He didn't take me along in the hansom—I ran alongside. No, I heard him say to Hopkins and Merriman that it wasn't a case for amateurs like Mr. Holmes and us."

Wiggins and Queenie gasped with rage.

"And what did Dr. Watson say about that?" asked Queenie.

But Lestrade had been more circumspect than to allow his remarks to be overheard by Dr. Watson, as I can confirm. Inspector Lestrade had his faults, but he would never wittingly offend a man of influence—he kept his criticisms of Mr. Holmes and the Irregulars to his subordinates, myself, and the unfortunate PC Boot, and to Merriman. Poor Boot came in for an ear-shaking tirade immediately afterwards, but that was Lestrade's way—he would bully his inferiors whilst sucking up to his superiors.

"Amateurs!" fumed Wiggins. "We're not amateurs—if Mr. Holmes was here we could have this case solved in a jiffy!"

"But he ain't," pointed out Shiner. "Poor Mr. Holmes is near death's door, after he got stabbed by Moriarty."

"So he is," said Wiggins, and he stared at the picture of the world's foremost detective for so long that the others began to feel restless.

"What are you staring like that for?" said Rosie. "You're making me feel all unnecessary, Wiggins."

"I was thinking," said Wiggins, "that Mr. Holmes is in that clinic in Switzerland, ain't he?"

"Yeh?" said Shiner.

"Yeh," said Wiggins. "And we're here."

Queenie sighed. "And we know what Wiggins means, don't we?" she said to the others.

"Elementary, my dear Queenie," said Wiggins. "We're going to show Inspector Lestrade he's wrong. We're going to solve the case of the missing documents—here, what's that?" he said, as Rosie slowly drew out the handkerchief which had been dropped by the old lady at the scene of the attack.

Sparrow took it from her. "Urgghh! Blood!" he said.

"Sir Alfred's blood, that's what," agreed Rosie. "I mopped him up wiv it—I couldn't give it back to the old girl, not when she'd done a bunk, could I?"

Wiggins pointed to a monogram which had been partially concealed by the congealed blood.

"That's an 'O'," he said. "Anyway, it's not a ladies' handkerchief, it's too big. What's 'O' for?"

"'Orace," said Shiner. "'Orrible 'Orace," Rosie said.

"'Orrible 'Orace from 'Ounslow," Sparrow went on. "It's a clue, Wiggins!"

"It might be," said Wiggins, who was getting ready to go out into the cold night. "But just now I'm going off to do what he'd do," he said, indicating the picture of Sherlock Holmes.

Queenie, Shiner, and Beaver also decided to go with Wiggins, but Rosie said she was too tired to face the icy fog, and Sparrow had his own plans.

"Not coming, Sparrer?" Beaver asked him.

"Nah," said Sparrow, but he didn't elaborate, so the four others left him behind with Rosie.

"How about you?" yawned Rosie as she saw that Sparrow was putting on his coat and ragged cloth-cap.

Sparrow lifted the silken handkerchief from the table.

"See this, Rosie girl," he said, slipping his hand into the silk, which parted to reveal a pocket.

"Funny kind of handkerchief," agreed Rosie.

"I've seen one like it once," Sparrow told her. "Down at the Alhambra."

"What? Down at the music-hall? Did some toff have it?"

"Nah," said Sparrow. "Some magician. And I'm going to ask about him."

"'Orrible 'Orace from 'Ounslow?" said Rosie, but Sparrow had slid out of the door into the yellow fog. "Magic again," she said, settling beside the fire. "Nasty magic too—I hope Sparrer don't run into that big bloke with the red beard."

* * * * * * *

In the thick fog, Wiggins led the little band to Merriman's.

"Why didn't Sparrer come along?" Shiner asked Beaver, as they walked shivering along the dimly-lit alleys.

"Dunno," said Beaver. "Sparrer's an odd kind of cove at times—he has his secrets, does Sparrer."

Queenie agreed. "He looked crafty, did little Sparrer," she said. "He's got something up his sleeve."

Shiner thought about it for a while. "Sparrer was staring at that handkerchief the old girl dropped," he said. "What do you think, Wiggins?"

"I dunno about Sparrer," said Wiggins as they reached Merriman's shop and peered through the window, "but I know there's been some dirty work going on here—see!"

And he pushed on the door, which had obviously been jemmied, for splinters and the wreckage of a lock littered the doorway. Great force had been used, and for a moment Wiggins held back.

Then he pushed forward.

"Mr. Merriman?" he called. "You all right, are you?"

He went ahead cautiously, trying to see into the gloom.

The others crowded behind him pushing him forward but unwilling to slip past him. Then there was a creaking, groaning sound from inside the shop, and Wiggins could make out a weird, swaying figure.

"What's that?" shrieked Queenie

Wiggins flinched, but a hollow voice came from the darkness. "—came back!" the voice cried, and it was Merriman. "I saw the same—but not the same!"

And with those barely-audible and totally mystifying words, the tobacconist crashed to the ground and was silent.

"It's Merriman!" yelled Wiggins, striking a match. "Here—see, the place has been done over!"

"How's Mr. Merriman?" asked Beaver.

Queenie screamed as she saw the pale face and the blank stare.

"He's a goner," said Wiggins. "Poor old Merriman—see, he didn't get a chance to blow his whistle," he went on, disentangling the silver whistle from the tobacconist's fingers. "Go on," he told Beaver. "The Law has to be brought into this."

He lit an undamaged oil-lamp and looked around the shop, whilst Queenie and Beaver summoned help. Drawers had been pulled from cupboards and hurled about in a frenzy, tables were overturned, and bowls and jugs smashed open; Wiggins, however, had been at the scene of a number of burglaries, and be saw something wrong about this one.

"They wasn't after his takings," he said.

He pointed to the shine of gold and. silver in the cashdrawer.

"Then what was they after?" demanded Beaver, who had returned after energetically blowing Merriman's police whistle.

"P'raps he knew!" whispered Queenie, indicating the corpse. "What was that he said just before he pegged out—something about it was the same and not the same, wasn't it?"

"And about someone coming back," agreed Wiggins.

"Mr. Holmes would puzzle it out if he was here," said Beaver. "He'd smoke his pipe, then he'd have a think, and he'd have it all worked out."

"So he would," admitted Wiggins. "An' that's what I ain't been doing!" he exclaimed, startling the others. "What—smoking?" said Queenie.

"I ain't been thinking!" said Wiggins. "I ain't been thinking about what they was after, that's what! Queenie, you and Shiner stay here to see the Law. Beaver, you're coming with me."

"Why?" yelled Queenie. "I don't want to stay with a body!"

"You do as you're told, girl," said Wiggins firmly. "Beaver and me are going after Sparrer, and if I'm right there's going to be more rough work tonight. No, Queenie, you talk to the Law when they get here."

"What if it's Inspector Lestrade?" said Queenie. "How can I tell an Inspector of Constables as you've gone out when there's a murder been done here, Arnold Wiggins?"

Wiggins could hear the clash of heavy boots on the pavement, and he knew he hadn't much time.

"Tell him Wiggins has a clue, that's what! Come on, Beaver!"

"But where are we going?" puffed Beaver, as they ran into the darkness.

"After Sparrer," said Wiggins.

"But where's Sparrer gone?" Beaver gasped.

"Into more trouble than he can handle!" said Wiggins, increasing his pace.

CHAPTER FOUR

"Wiggins ain't the only one who knows Mr. Holmes's methods," Sparrow assured himself as he reached the side door of the Alhambra music-hall. "I was the one what found the clue, so I'm the one what's going to follow it up," he went on, forgetting Rosie's part in obtaining the white silk handkerchief with the odd pocket.

"What do you want?" demanded the doorman as Sparrow entered the side-door. "This door's for artistes and such—hop it, you."

"I'm Sparrer," said Sparrow. "Don't you remember me, Bert?"

Bert the doorman looked closer, and saw that beneath the swathings of ragged scarf and the over-large cap was an old friend.

"Yeh," he said. "What do you want, then?'"

"You know about magic things, don't you, Bert? See 'ere—what's this, then?" said Sparrow, passing Bert the bloodstained handkerchief.

"Had a nosebleed, Sparrer?" asked Bert, examining the square of silk.

"Nah—accident. How about it, Bert? That pocket thing in it—recognise it?"

"Easy," said Bert. He demonstrated for Sparrow. "I've seen it done a hundred times on stage. The illusionist holds the egg or whatever in his hand, over goes the trick handkerchief, a wave of the other hand to distract them, and away goes the egg. He calls it magic, but it's the oldest trick in the book."

"Who does?" said Sparrow.

"Who does what?" said Bert.

"Who calls it magic?" Sparrow persisted.

Bert sighed. "Didn't you see who's on at the hall this week? Orlov! The Great Orlov he calls himself. And he's not bad either, isn't Orlov, even if he does use the oldest trick in the book with this here handkerchief. See—it's got his initial on—'O' for Orlov."

Sparrow was staggered. He had followed up a clue, but here was more than he had expected, far more. He had expected the doorman to give him some ideas about who might have used the handkerchief, and here was Bert telling him that its owner was now appearing at this very music hall!

"Wiggins'll be sick!" he couldn't help saying.

"How's that?" said Bert.

"Nothing, Bert!" Sparrow told him. "Is this bloke—the Great Orlov—still here?"

Bert shook his head. "Finished and gone. Tonight was his last appearance. D'you want me to hang on to his hankie in case he comes back?"

"Nah," said Sparrow, his heart beating faster. "Tell me where he lives and I'll take it to him—maybe it's worth a tanner to him, it being part of his act."

Bert laughed and gave Sparrow an address a few streets away.

"There's no flies on you, me old cock-sparrer!" he called as Sparrow ran out into the thick swirling fog. "I hope he does get his tanner, but I don't fancy his chances. Orlov ain't full of the milk of human kindness, but then he's a foreigner, ain't he?"

Sparrow pelted through alleyways and down narrow, cobbled streets, and dodged the occasional cab that splattered mud over him. And all the time he found himself getting nearer to a particular alleyway which he knew.

"I've been here before!" said Sparrow, peering into the ill-lit alleyway at the rear of the street where Orlov lived.

Sparrow's heart pounded as he approached the end house.

"That's the one Bert said he lives at," thought Sparrow. "And round the back is where that red-bearded bloke vanished—it's like Rosie said, it's all magic, only nastier. I wonder if Orlov's in?"

He peered through the windows at the front of the small, terraced house, but though there was a candle guttering in the parlour, he could see no sign of the illusionist.

"I'll go round the back," Sparrow decided.

Quietly and stealthily Sparrow slid down the alleyway until he located the yard door of the end house. It was open. Sparrow hesitated. Should he investigate, or should he report to Wiggins and the others?

Sparrow peered inside. There was a patch of light from the back door of the house—the back door was open too. He shivered with more than the cold of the swirling fog. "Nah," he thought. "I'll go back for—what's that?"

Heavy footsteps rang on the cobbles of the alley.

Someone was coming!

Sparrow almost passed out with terror. He felt his heart fluttering madly and he was sure that the big figure that loomed nearer and nearer could hear it. Without another thought, Sparrow darted through the yard and into the house—there was no time to look for a hiding place: he was into the house as the metal-tipped boots rang in the backyard.

"Where!" groaned Sparrow as he surveyed the bleak little room.

On a battered table were gleaming tools and bundles of brownish-looking candles, together with a number of iron canisters; three chairs and a chest made up the rest of the furniture. And, from another part of the house—from somewhere at the front—Sparrow heard a thick foreign voice calling.

"Bukovsky?" it called, then there was a gabble of some weird language that sounded as if the speaker had his mouth full of cabbage.

"In there." Sparrow told himself, moving swiftly.

It was a built-in cupboard, large enough for Sparrow and not much more. Sparrow had it open in a second, and then he was wriggling into an assortment of illusionist's equipment and old clothes, certain that he must be found and murdered within seconds.

In his last glimpses of the back room, however, he had noticed a number of things. One was a large revolver on one of the chairs, together with a box of ammunition. Another was that the cupboard which sheltered him contained some familiar items, including a red beard and a ladies' winter outfit; and there was one more thing that in itself convinced Sparrow of the danger he was in.

It was a shiny black leather despatch-case, and on it was the golden insignia of a Crown.

"It was him!" Sparrow whispered. "The old girl—it was him!" Everything began to fall into place, although it was several minutes before Sparrow was calm enough to work it out.

Even then, he found himself listening to a long, monotonous conversation in a language he didn't understand; all the time, sweating with terror and with the red beard finding its way under his collar as he burrowed into the Great Orlov's equipment!

Sparrow wished ten thousand times that he had not been so adventurous. He told himself that he had been stupid to be jealous of Wiggins and go off on his own. He promised himself faithfully that if he didn't sneeze and alert the big man, he would never, never try to be a detective again.

But after a while, even terror became boring, and Sparrow listened more carefully to what the two men were saying. Their conversation seemed to last for hours—days.

Every so often, Sparrow heard a name or a phrase repeated, so he was able to work out the men's names. Orlov wasn't Orlov, he was Orlovitch. And the big bloke was Bukovsky.

Then Sparrow grew more alert.

"What?" he thought, as a familiar-sounding name, which a foreign accent couldn't entirely conceal was repeated. "He said Sir Alfred Connyngham!"

And then, amazingly, the two men began to converse in English!

"In one week," said Orlovitch. "And when he dies, we will make the Revolution!"

"When who dies?" wondered Sparrow, concentrating harder now. "Are they going to do Sir Alfred again?"

Sparrow stored every word as gradually the men went over the details of their plan. The trouble was, however, that he was becoming sleepy.

Whether it was—the lack of air in the cupboard combined with the build up of body-heat, or whether Sparrow was just plain tired after being out in the bitter cold since dawn that day—the fact was that he fell asleep.

He heard a great. deal, but he was fortunate enough to miss the worst threat to his continued existence.

"And the props from your act?" said Bukovsky, who was packing away the tools and apparatus on the table. "The despatch case and the clothes—what of them?"

Orlov shook his head.

"Leave them. From tonight, Orlov is finished. Dropping the handkerchief marked me as Orlov, and the trail must lead to here. A few more clues of the same kind won't harm us—we leave here now for good. Come!"

Bukovsky blew out the candles,

Then his sharp hearing almost led to the finding of the sleeping boy. "You hear something?" he said to Orlovitch.

Orlovitch listened. "Nothing."

"Something like—like a cat purring?" persisted Bukovsky. Orlovitch shook his head impatiently.

"We've waited long enough—delay is dangerous. Come!"

All of this passed Sparrow by as he dozed for another hour or so—the time it took Wiggins and Beaver to find him. Sparrow snored gently, and the streets around him grew quieter until there was absolute silence in the dark old house.

Sparrow heard Beaver's voice first.

"Ouch!" he cried as he crashed into a fallen chair, for the house was in darkness.

"Shut up!" whispered Wiggins.

"Why? There ain't no one here," said Beaver.

"You hope!" said Wiggins, striking a match. "No, they've scarpered."

"And how about poor old Sparrer?" whispered Beaver, as he thought of what might have happened to his friend.

"Yeh," agreed Wiggins, lighting a pair of candies. "What's that?" he gasped, as he heard a faint, regular sound.

"What?" yelled Beaver, jumping away from him.

"I can hear something—low and horrible!"

"Orlov!" whispered Beaver. "'Orrible Orlov!"

"It's coming from in there," whispered Wiggins.

"Let's get out of here!" yelled Beaver.

"Let me out first!" yelled back Sparrow.

"Yowwww!" roared Wiggins and Beaver, heading for the back-door.

"It's me!" yelled Sparrow. "Me—Sparrer!"

"Where?" cried Beaver.

"Where do you think!" yelled back Sparrow. "In the blinking cupboard!"

It took only a moment or two to disentangle Sparrow from Orlov's stage props and Bukovsky's beard, and not many minutes for Sparrow to tell his tale, and an alarming story it was.

It raised as many questions as it answered, but at least one part of the mystery was explained.

Wiggins examined the female clothes, then the shopping-bag, and the red beard, and, finally, Sir.Alfred Connyngham's despatch-case.

"It was all a trick," he said. "Illusions, as you would say."

"'Course it was!" said Sparrow. "That's what the Great Orlov does for a living, ain't it? He dressed up as an old girl, then his pal Bukovsky comes along with his red beard and his cosh to make it look as if he's knocking her about."

"But he ain't," said Beaver.

Wiggins agreed. "Then when Bukovsky runs off, the old girl gets taken into Merriman's—but she's Orlovitch, so when he's alone, he gets his own clothes out of the shopping-bag, does a quick change, then he hops it outside."

"Wiv the despatch case in the carpet-bag he had all the time folded up," finished Sparrow.

"And now it's empty," said Beaver.

"'Course it is," said Sparrow. "They was after the papers inside it, wasn't they? And now they've got them, and there's going to be all kinds of trouble!"

Wiggins and Beaver listened to what Sparrow could remember of all he had heard. It was a story of violence and outrage, bloodshed and revolution, anarchy and war.

"And it starts," said Sparrow, "when they blows up this Archduke. That's what Orlovitch said when he wasn't speaking in that heathen language. 'Bukovsky,' he tells this big bloke, 'we will dynamite the Archduke in just one week'!"

"Dynamite him!" breathed Beaver.

"Yes," said Sparrow. "Somewhere near a chimney or something, but I didn't gather much about that, it was all in heathen."

"And what else did you hear?" demanded Wiggins. "Before you fell asleep, Sparrer."

"You'd have been stifled in there too, Wiggins!" exclaimed Sparrow.

"Didn't I listen till I was nearly choked—and wiv a red beard tickling me neck all the time? What if I'd have sneezed? That big ugly bloke would've murdered me, he would!"

Wiggins soothed the angry little Cockney and got the rest of his incredible story. Sparrow had been drowsy for much of the time, and Orlovitch and Bukovsky had only occasionally spoken in English. But Sparrow had heard over and over again the same phrases.

"'Three tons', so Orlovitch said," Sparrow recalled. "Him and Bukovsky said it maybe half-a-dozen times. And they're going to do him today week."

"Next Monday," said Beaver. "Cor!"

"Near a chimney?" said Wiggins.

"Yeh," said Sparrow. "Wiv three tons of dynamite. Then he said, clear as you like in English, 'They'll not be looking for us, disguised as we will be, Bukovsky—Long Live the Revolution!'"

In turn, Wiggins described how he had used Mr. Holmes's methods to find Sparrow, and they were all about to congratulate themselves on solving the case of the Missing Despatch Case when they heard loud sounds from the front and back of the house.

"It's that big bloke what done Merriman in!" gasped Beaver.

"What coshed Sir Alfred!" groaned Sparrow.

"What Orlovitch pals up with!" cried Wiggins.

Then Wiggins recognised a loud, authoritative voice ordering men to have their revolvers ready.

"Lestrade!" said Wiggins. "The Law's here!"

"Just when we found who really stole the despatch case," said Sparrow.

"And why," added Beaver.

"You in there!" bellowed a stern voice. "Hands on your heads and come out quiet-like, if you understand English, and if you don't, look at this, what'll blow you to Kingdom Come if you resists arrest!"

The snout of a large pistol was thrust through the door.

"Why, it's a gang of street urchins!" bellowed a constable. "Sir, I think it's those ragamuffins again!"

Inspector Lestrade poked his nose into the room above another large pistol. He sighed.

"I thought they'd be here," he said. "Why am I plagued by amateurs when I'm in the middle of the most important case of my whole career? See to them, Sergeant," he told me (for I was still on duty that evening). "And then get rid of them!"

CHAPTER FIVE

I pointed out to Inspector Lestrade that he was being unfair to Sparrow, but the Inspector became quite irate when I attempted to argue with him.

The way he saw it was that Rosie was in the wrong for tampering with evidence in the first place. Inspector Lestrade held that she shouldn't have kept the handkerchief once Orlovitch—in his disguise as an old woman—had dropped it. It was my view though that, but for Sparrow's quick-wittedness, the trail leading to Orlovitch and Bukovsky would have been impossible to follow.

"Nonsense!" Inspector Lestrade declared to me, when the Baker Street Irregulars had been sent off with a flea in their (not very clean) ears. "Routine police methods would have brought about the same results, but quicker! Now, don't let me hear anymore about those wretched ragamuffins and their escapades! I have informed my superiors that I expect to arrest these revolutionaries before long, and I have Sir Alfred's complete confidence. As for this nonsense about three tons of dynamite—whoever heard of such rubbish? Why, three tons of dynamite would be enough to blow up half of Central London, and to my certain knowledge these anarchists use only small bombs for their villainies!"

And so, as far as Inspector Lestrade was concerned, that was that.

He dismissed all that Sparrow had heard as so much nonsense—the product of his dreams while he slept in

Orlovitch's cupboard. The important thing, so far as the Inspector saw it, was to guard the Archduke who was the central figure in the plot.

There was no secrecy about the coming visit to this country of Archduke Alexander of Rosnia. All the newspapers had reported that he was paying a ceremonial visit to Her Majesty; of course, the real purpose of his visit had not been disclosed. Orlovitch and Bukovsky were now in possession of the secret reasons behind the Archduke's stay at Windsor with Her Majesty, and they were determined to prevent him from fulfilling them.

"The Archduke's the target of these anarchists," Inspector Lestrade told me. "Where he goes, I go—that's the way to do police work, Hopkins. Safety first!"

"And Orlovitch and Bukovsky, sir?" I said to Inspector Lestrade.

"Every officer in the force is on the lookout for them!" said the Inspector. "Photographs of the anarchists will be displayed at every station in London by this time tomorrow. I'll have them in twenty-four hours!"

Wiggins thought otherwise. When he saw the late newspapers the following day, he said:

"Don't they know they're lookin' for a couple of expert illusionists? Does Lestrade think they're going to walk past his bobbies with a revolver in one hand and a smoking bomb in the other with a label on their hats sayin' 'Anarchists'?"

Beaver, who had provided the late edition of the morning's news, gazed at the breathless account of the night's adventures: 'VICIOUS ASSAULT ON PEER OF THE REALM! TOBACCONIST SLAIN IN ANARCHIST PLOT! INSPECTOR LESTRADE SPEAKS OF IMMINENT ARREST!'

Together the rest of the Baker Street Boys read how the police had been summoned to the scene of the attack on Sir Alfred Connyngham, and then how Inspector Lestrade and his detectives had linked that outrage with the murderous attack on Merriman.

"'S'trewth!" whistled Wiggins when he had finished. "Not a word about the Archduke. Lestrade's pursuing his enquiries amongst the theatrical fraternity, so it says here, but it don't say it was Sparrer that found the Great Orlov. And not a word about any missing documents either."

Nor was there any mention of a plot against the life of Archduke Alexander in the newspapers during the next few days. Wiggins and the others impatiently read every account of Lestrade's progress—though that wasn't much—and every day their annoyance grew.

"He still says an arrest is imminent," said Wiggins. "What's imminent? When he can't think of anything else to say to the reporters."

His gaze came to rest as it often did on the stern features of Sherlock Holmes.

"I wonder what he'd do?" he muttered.

Queenie was quite sure about it. "Well, for a start he wouldn't let Lestrade warn him off, not when he'd got a bunch of clues like what we've got."

"We ain't got no clues," said Shiner. "Only what Sparrer heard.

"And what's those but clues!" blazed Sparrow. "We know when they're going to blow up the Archduke—next Monday. And I did hear them gabble on about three tons of something and about chimneys!"

Wiggins was thoughtful.

"See how Lestrade looks at it," he told them. "He thinks Sparrer's barmy—didn't he ask if we thought the Archduke was going to stand on a chimney while Bukovsky and Orlovitch stood around at the bottom ready to blow him sky-high with three tons of dynamite?"

"So he did," agreed Beaver. "And it is barmy!"

Reluctantly, they agreed that they had nothing to go on. It seemed that for them anyway the case of the Missing Despatch Case was over, but the next day brought a summons that was to change matters completely. It came in the form of a note from

Dr. Watson.

"I have important news for you," the note read. "Bring the rest of the Irregulars and make sure they wipe their feet on the mat, or Mrs Hudson will be displeased. J. H. Watson, M.D."

"Dr. Watson wants us?" said Queenie. "All of us?"

"With clean boots," said Wiggins. "Or his housekeeper will be mad."

"What does he want?" demanded Rosie.

Wiggins spent another moment or two gazing at the picture of Sherlock Holmes.

"I got just about half an idea," he said, but he would say no more.

Mrs Hudson supervised the entry of the Irregulars with a careful and hostile eye, but they gave her no cause for offence.

"Ah—come into the study!" declared Dr. Watson. "It will be quite suitable in the circumstances," and the children gazed about them in awe as they looked around the most famous collection of criminal relics in the world.

They saw Mr. Sherlock Holmes's pipes, his microscope with a slide ready to be examined in it, his fencing-foils, his pistols on the mantelpiece, and even his slippers.

"Phew!" muttered Wiggins, who was almost overcome with awe, but not quite.

"I'll be brief," said Dr. Watson. "I have here a telegram from Mr. Sherlock Holmes—"

"From Mr. Holmes!" cried Wiggins. "But he's on his death-bed, sir!"

"Poor Mr. Holmes!" wept Rosie. "He's a goner, ain't he?"

"Now, now!" cried Dr. Watson. "No tears, if you please. They're quite unnecessary. I'm delighted to say that Mr. Holmes is making a steady recovery—"

"Smashing!" yelled Wiggins.

"Hurray!" yelled Shiner, with the others joining in delightedly.

Dr. Watson smiled at their enthusiasm, but his face became stern once more.

"Really, that's quite enough interruptions," he told the Baker Street Boys. "Mr. Holmes is still a very sick man, but when I heard lately that there was some improvement in his condition, I took it upon myself to inform him of the difficulties In the case you became involved in. And this is his reply. Listen."

And Dr. Watson read out the message from Mr. Sherlock Holmes to the children:

"'In the matter of the disappearance of Sir Alfred Connyngham's Despatch Case, kindly inform the Baker Street Irregulars that their instincts are right. Lestrade has not the imagination to follow up their valuable clues, so they must busy themselves in the matter. Be sure to remind them above all that in this case things are not always what they seem'." Dr. Watson folded the telegram and put it in his pocket.

"I said it, didn't I?" said Sparrow. "It's all magic and faking, that's what."

"As Mr. Holmes points out," agreed Dr. Watson.

"So we're back on the case," announced Wiggins, once more gazing around the room at the Master's possessions.

"And so you should be," said Dr. Watson. "Lestrade and young Sergeant Hopkins have been to see me more than once in the past few days, and it became clear to me that they were at a dead end. I took the liberty of informing Mr. Holmes of this case, and you have heard his reply. I can tell you that Inspector Lestrade is very worried at his lack of progress, and that meanwhile he travels everywhere with the Archduke to ensure his safety."

"He's got a hope, with Orlovitch and Bukovsky around," said Wiggins.

"Those two are too crafty for Inspector Lestrade."

"No doubt," said Dr. Watson. "But where will you start, Wiggins?"

"Number 41 Park Lane, sir."

"Where did you say? Ah, of course! At Sir Alfred Connyngham's residence."

"That's right, sir," said Wiggins. "We read as how Sir Alfred's recovering at his London residence, and maybe he's well enough to listen to a bit of sense now. Tomorrow's Monday, and that's when this Archduke bloke's due to be murdered. We ain't got no time to waste."

"My sentiments exactly!" cried Dr. Watson. "It could be Mr. Holmes himself speaking!"

The Baker Street Boys were in a cheerful mood as they reached the railings in front of Sir Alfred's Park Lane home, but their optimism was soon dampened. It was a murky evening once more, with a heavy fall of rain and sleet, and what they heard on their arrival made matters worse. "Here!" called a loud, authoritative voice. "You lot—get away from those gates—scarper, fast!"

A large police constable in a glistening cape loomed out of the darkness to confront Wiggins and the others. Another equally large policeman patrolled the grounds inside the railings.

"Who's there?" called the second policeman. "Pack of kids!"

"What they after?"

"We've got to see Sir Alfred Connyngham!" called Wiggins.

"Who!" cried the first policeman.

"It's true!" Queenie yelled. "It's a matter of life and death!"

"They're going to blow up the Archduke," said Rosie. "And we know Sir Alfred—he bought some flowers from me the night he was attacked!" The second policeman now examined the urchins.

"What an 'orrible lot!" he said. "Get off—scarper!"

"But we helped wiv the investigation!" cried Wiggins, stung by this unpleasant remark. "We helped Inspector Lestrade after Sir Alfred got done by those two anarchists!"

"So you're those meddling busybody kids!" said the first policeman. "I heard about you concealing evidence and getting in the way of the Law. And I'll tell you this: if you don't clear off in ten seconds, you'll find yourselves in a cell for the night!" Wiggins led the others away.

Only Sparrow could find an answer for the two burly police-constables. "I hope that big foreign bloke comes round here!" he yelled. "Then you'll know who's telling the truth!"

A bellow of anger greeted this, and the Baker Street Boys took to their heels. Down one well-lit street they raced, and then Wiggins darted into a dark alleyway.

"Now what?" said Sparrow. "We're finished, ain't we?"

"Who says?" demanded Wiggins. "Here, Beaver and Queenie, you two come wiv me—wait here, you others."

"Why?" they demanded.

"'Cos you're too little to go where we're going."

"Where's that?" said Queenie.

"Where the servants goes for a drink," said Wiggins. "I saw a public house—just round the back here—it's the nearest to Sir Alfred's, so that's where his staff'll be drinking when they drinks."

"And then what?" demanded Beaver, as they came to a brightly-lit and noisy public house called the Wheatsheaf.

"Dunno," said Wiggins. "But it's better'n being chased off by bobbies. Maybe we can get a message through to him, who knows?"

"And maybe we'll get a thick ear for being nosey," said Queenie. Wiggins grinned.

"Do you think Mr. Holmes would let himself be scared off?"

Sparrow, Shiner, and Rosie were not left long in doubt, for Wiggins and the others were back within minutes.

"Wiggins done it!" cried Beaver. "He's gone and worked out the clue!"

"What, where Orlovitch and Bukovsky are hiding?" said Shiner.

"Nah!" said Queenie. "Where Sir Alfred's gone!"

"But he's round the corner in Park Lane," said Sparrow. "Ain't he?"

"No he ain't," announced Wiggins. "I saw one of the chambermaids; she'd had a few gins, and she let it slip before the underbutler could shut her up that Sir Alfred's gone to his country residence."

"So what's the bobbies for if he ain't in Park Lane?" demanded Shiner.

"All bluff!" Wiggins said. "The bobbies outside think he's inside, but he ain't—he's at The Chimneys."

"At the what?" said Sparrow. "Yeah!" he yelled suddenly. "It's the name of a place—they calls big houses fancy names. Of course—it weren't one chimney."

"It was The Chimneys, near Newgate Village in Hertfordshire, more'n twenty miles on the train from here," agreed Wiggins. "And that's where we're going!"

They had reckoned, however, without the train timetables.

* * * * * *

"First train out to Newgate?" they heard at Euston Station. "You'll have a long wait. That's the milk-train leaving here at five-thirty A.M."

Sparrow groaned in dismay, and Shiner tried to argue with the ticket-clerk, but all he got was a threat of a call to the railway police; and so it was Wiggins who had to take the lead once more.

"Home, all of you, excepting Sparrer," he said. "We'll wait for the first train and get out to see Sir Alfred."

There was a howl of protest from the others until Wiggins pointed out that their total wealth came to one shilling and tenpence, which was exactly the cost of two single fares to Newgate Village Station. Wiggins went on:

"I'm going 'cos I say so, and Sparrer's coming with me 'cos—he knows the clues, that's why," and this had to satisfy the rest of the Boys.

It was an uncomfortable night for the two of them, but they were hardy and thought nothing of it. An hour before dawn the steam-train clanked into Newgate Village Station, they got out, and a sleepy porter gave them directions to The Chimneys.

"How long we been walking now?" said Sparrow, an hour later.

Dawn was breaking through low, hazy clouds, but fortunately there was no rain or snow. Wiggins consulted his watch.

"Dunno," he said. "It's stopped again. We've gotta be near, though, we been walking for hours along these lanes."

They tramped on and rounded a narrow bend at the top of a steep climb. An imposing wall began beside the road, and a little way down the hill was a set of iron gates decorated with a coat of arms.

Through the trees, Wiggins and Sparrow saw their destination.

The Chimneys was an old, rambling mansion with Elizabethan timbers and red brick, but its most prominent feature was a remarkable number of high chimneys in its roofs. Getting over the gates presented no problems. "I hope their dogs isn't savage," said Wiggins, as be helped Sparrow down.

"And their servants isn't too handy with guns," agreed Sparrow.

But they reached the huge porch without attracting any attention whatsoever. Before them was a pair of high wooden doors, again engraved with a coat of arms; and a bell-pull on a black iron chain.

"Here goes," said Wiggins, pulling on the chain. There was a deep, sombre clanging from the house. Dogs woke up on the instant. A deep baying sound left the two boys wishing they were back in London; and they felt their knees turn to jelly when a pair of servants opened the doors and confronted them with wide-mouthed shotguns and the snarling teeth of half-a-dozen hounds.

"Who're you two young villains!" demanded a burly, older man.

"We ain't villains or any such things!" cried Wiggins. "We got a warning for Sir Alfred Connyngham—"

"Don't you come with threats for Sir Alfred!" cried the second man. "We got dogs for your kind!"

"But we got clues about the Archduke!" Sparrow called, seeing that they were being totally misunderstood. "We came to help—we're the ones what looked after Sir Alfred when he got done on Monday last!"

"Was you?" said the second man, but the other one didn't want to hear anymore. "Some ragamuffins did help his Lordship, that I know."

"You two knows too much," he decided. "Lock 'em up, Yates, and send for the bobbies like Inspector Lestrade said we should if there was trouble—come on, you two, I've got a storeroom with iron bars till the Law arrives! Sir Alfred ain't here, so we'll do what seems best."

"But it's a matter of life and death!" Wiggins tried to say. "We know these anarchists is goin' to try to kill the Archduke!"

A growl from the older man was his only answer, but another voice came through the sullen snapping of the dogs, and it was obviously someone who expected to be obeyed:

"What's this about the Archduke?" called a young man. "Wait, Roberts—who are these boys?"

Roberts wasn't given a chance to explain. In a few short sentences, Wiggins was able to convince the young man—who wasn't much older than he himself—that he was acting in good faith.

"Best put them somewhere secure, sir!" cried Roberts.

"In my father's absence, I'll decide what's to be done!" cried the young man. "And you, Roberts, can make a start by bringing some breakfast. These boys look famished, and if I'm any judge they've walked from the station this morning. Yates, clear those confounded hounds away!" lie went on. "Now, you two—I'm Freddie Connyngham. Sir Alfred's not here, as you've gathered, and I want an explanation from you both. But first let me tell you I know about last Monday's attack. I'm grateful for what you did to help my father, but I realise that your business must be of the utmost urgency—so fire away, you have my entire attention!"

Wiggins and Sparrow took turns in describing what they knew. And then, over breakfast, Wiggins came to his conclusions.

"We know Orlovitch and Bukovsky are going to try to

murder the Archduke," he said. "And we know that Sir Alfred's involved. But we can't square up the other things—not three tons of dynamite, unless it's to blow up this place."

Freddie Connyngham whistled loudly.

"By Jove, I hope not! Now, let's get a few things straight," he went on. "The Archduke isn't here, nor, of course, is my father. They're due here, though, at about ten this morning, by special train, along with the Foreign Ministers of four more countries, and I can quite see that these anarchists would wish all of them blown sky-high. But I can assure you this place is too well-guarded for any desperadoes to enter—they wouldn't get past the dogs. As for three tons—"

He was interrupted by Roberts, bearing further supplies of food. "The Three Tuns, did you say, sir?" said Roberts.

Freddie Connyngham dismissed the interruption.

"I wasn't talking to you, Roberts,'" he said irritably, but Sparrow had suddenly sprung to his feet and hared off after the servant.

"Here!" the others heard him call to Roberts. "You said 'The Three Tuns'—why'd you say that?"

"So he did," said Freddie Connyngham slowly. "And I can answer that myself!"

"It's a public house!" called Sparrow triumphantly. "And it's near a bridge—"

"Over which the special train must pass to get onto our private siding!" Freddie Connyngham said, his face growing pale. "Of course—you didn't hear the anarchists talking about a weight of explosives, you heard them naming a rendezvous!"

Wiggins shook his watch. Sparrow heard a clock chime.

"'S'trewth!" he cried. "We've got an hour, no more! And it took us a lot more'n that to get here!"

"The last clue," said Wiggins. "It all falls into place, like a pattern, as Mr. Holmes would say."

"Arm yourselves, Roberts—Yates! Send the trap for help! Bring some of the men from the home farm—and fetch me a revolver at once!"

"Phew!" muttered Sparrow in admiration. "Revolvers!"

"We're dealing with murderers!" said Wiggins. "And they'd blow us up too if they could! Ain't we going in the trap?" he asked Freddie.

But the shortest way by far was not by road.

"We're going along our private railway line," declared Freddie Connyngham. "It won't take us more than half-an-hour with luck to get to The Three Tuns, but heaven help us if we're late, for the bridge there crosses a gorge a hundred feet deep, and no doubt the anarchists have mined it!"

Out of the house and into the woods went the boys and Freddie Connyngham, followed by Yates and Roberts and an assortment of delighted hounds. They ran along the track of the private line that linked The Chimneys with the public railway system. Before long, they had left the servants far behind.

"Keep going!" Wiggins called to Sparrow. "Got a stitch!" he moaned.

"And me, old man," groaned Freddie.

"Run it off!" growled Wiggins, lengthening his stride. "How far now?" he asked Freddie.

"A mile—maybe a bit more!" panted Freddie Connyngham.

"We're cutting it fine," said Wiggins. "Come on!"

But Freddie Connyngham was no athlete, and Sparrow was near exhaustion after his sleepless night.

"I'll take the revolver," decided Wiggins, grabbing the weapon from Freddie's nerveless hand. "You two follow!"

"No need!" called Freddie, as Wiggins began to draw ahead. "Look!" A small gang of railway workmen were eating their morning bread-and-cheese beside the track.

"'Morning, sir!" they called, looking in puzzlement at Freddie Connyngham in the company of a pair of boys, one of whom was holding a large revolver, "Need any help, sir?" said their ganger cautiously.

"That bogey!" cried Freddie. "Can you get it on to the lines?"

"We could," agreed the ganger. "If that's your wish, sir!"

In a few moments, the three of them were bowling along

the line at a high speed, and within five minutes or so Freddie hauled on the brake.

"We're coming to the regular passenger line," he said. "The Three Tuns is only a few hundred yards away—and there's the bridge! Here, let's push the bogey off the track and take a look."

It was a wooden bridge, sturdy enough for occasional traffic, but without the massive strength of the iron railway bridges Wiggins and Sparrow knew in London.

Far below they could see a rushing stream strewn with jagged boulders. Wiggins gulped.

"Cor!" murmured Sparrow. "If the train was to—"

"Exactly!" said Freddie, who had recovered his poise. "But we're here and we can warn the driver to stop—come on!"

As the boys approached the bridge, however, Freddie paused. "That's odd," he said.

"What's odd?" said Sparrow.

"Those railwaymen—track inspectors by the look of them," said Wiggins. "Now why should there be two gangs out on the same length of track—look, on the far side of the bridge. Only two of 'em," he continued slowly. "One a big bloke, an' one small and nasty. And both of them dressed like railway workers."

"Yeh," agreed Sparrow. "It's them!"

"Who?" demanded Freddie Connyngham, as the two men on the far side of the bridge noticed that they had been spotted.

"The Great Orlov!" said Wiggins. "And the bloke with the red beard! Watch out! They're shooting!"

Shots rang out, and the boys dived for cover.

"Then they have mined the bridge!" cried Freddie. "And they'll pin us down till the train comes, and it's all up with father and the Archduke!"

"And a few foreign ministers and suchlike," agreed Sparrow. "And Inspector Lestrade," he added thoughtfully.

Of course, it would have been the end of me too had the boys not acted, for I was on the special train with Inspector Lestrade. We were keeping a sharp lookout for anything suspicious, and the Inspector had even placed a couple of his men in the cab of the engine to watch the track. But all our precautions would have been in vain had not young Wiggins employed that combination of caution and daring which was so reminiscent of the Master.

"Here!" yelled Wiggins, as bullets whistled around his ears. "Get the bogey back on the track—they can't hit us back there!"

It was true. The bogey was out of range of the revolvers, and it took only a little time for the boys to wrestle the heavy bogey back on to the track. Desperation lent them additional strength, but when it was in place both Sparrow and Freddie were baffled.

"Now what?" said Sparrow. "I'm not going over that bridge on this thing, 'cos I'll get me head blown off."

"It's a diabolical risk," agreed Freddie, "but I'm game!" Wiggins was already providing the answer to their dilemma.

"Here!" he said, indicating a pile of railway sleepers, massive timbers stored as replacements for those that rotted. "Get a dozen of these in front, then we'll be safe!"

And so it proved.

With only a minute or so to spare before the special train reached the mined bridge, the three boys had erected a barricade of heavy logs before them.

"Faster!" yelled Wiggins, as Sparrow and Freddie and he pumped with the last of their strength on the handles of the bogey. "Come on!"

Bullets thudded into the heavy timbers.

"We're on the bridge!" panted Freddie. "Not far now!"

"Then those anarchists can shoot us as we go by!" yelled Sparrow.

"Nah!" groaned Wiggins, whose own energies were practically used up.

"We'll jump just after the bridge and dodge into the woods—that's the best we can do!"

"But what about the train—it'll hit the bogey!" panted Sparrow.

"Better that than being blown sky-high!" said Freddie grimly.

"Well, Wiggins—well, Sparrow—good luck!"

Then they were all leaping from the bogey only yards short of where the gunmen lay.

As they jumped, Wiggins caught sight of an electrical battery and a pair of wires leading to the bridge. He also heard a roar of rage from Bukovsky. "Well," he said as he landed on a gravel incline. "We did what we could—and I hope it's enough."

It was. The three boys were too much concerned with their own immediate problems to take in what was happening, but I was very much aware of the events of the next half-minute.

A heavy shock ran along the train, hurling foreign ministers and senior policemen, to say nothing of important politicians, across their carriages.

The only casualty was the Archduke, who suffered a slight cut on his nose; he gained it whilst trimming his moustache in the bathroom of the special train.

He recovered sufficiently to join in the thanks and congratulations of Sir Alfred Connyngham, when he and the other dignitaries were told of their escape from death, and the part the boys had played in saving them. "You have saved my life twice over," said Sir Alfred beside the railway track, watched by a humbled Inspector Lestrade. "I know everyone here joins me in this heartfelt expression of gratitude—we all owe our lives, and the peace of Europe itself to you. I can tell you now that the Archduke Alexander is in this country to sign a treaty with the Foreign Ministers of four other nations, and because of your gallantry the signing will take place at The Chimneys. What do you say, Lestrade?" he said, turning to the Inspector.

And there, in front of the distinguished assembly, Wiggins and Sparrow listened to Inspector Lestrade's congratulations too. I later heard him say that regular police enquiries would have done just as well; but the truth is different.

There was some consolation for the Inspector, however.

Bukovsky and Orlovitch were later arrested in yet another of their disguises at Dover as they tried to board a steamer for the Continent. Wiggins had the last word:

"They didn't get away with it this time," he said. "Mind you, even Inspector Lestrade finally worked out that in the case of the Disappearing Despatch Case, things wasn't always what they seemed."

ABOUT THE AUTHOR

BRIAN (NEVILLE) BALL was born on June 19, 1932, in Cheshire, England. Much of his substantial body of novels—science fiction, supernatural, detective thrillers, and childrens' fiction—beginning in the early 1960s and continuing to date—was produced whilst Ball simultaneously pursued an academic career as a Lecturer in English at Doncaster College of Education, and whilst he was Visiting Professor to the University of British Colombia, Vancouver.

Like many of his British contemporaries, Ball began by writing science fiction short stories for *New Worlds* and *Science Fantasy*, but very quickly made the transition to full-length sf novels, beginning with *Sundog* in 1965. His early sf novels, whilst action-packed adventure stories, were also rich in metaphysical speculation, qualities that quickly brought him international recognition, His series of children's books, ranging from nursery to teenage titles, were equally successful.

Of his adult science fiction novels, of especial note was his trilogy about an ancient Galactic Federation, *Timepiece (*1968), *Timepivot* (1970), and *Planet Probability* (1973). By 1971 he had began to diversify into supernatural novels with considerable success, and in 1974 his first detective novel, *Death of a Low-Handicap Man*, was published to wide acclaim. This novel is currently in print from Wildside, and a recent new sequel, *Death on the Driving Range* (2009), is scheduled to appear from the Borgo Press, along with the best of his supernatural novels, beginning with *Mark of the Beast* and *The Evil at Monteine*.

In 2004 Ball resumed writing short stories for Philip Harbottle's *Fantasy Adventures* collections, published by Wildside Press, of which "Dark Peak" (*FA #9*) and "Seeing Flynn" (*FA #13*) stand out.

Also in 2004, Ball was commissioned to write a new *Space: 1999* novel explaining the mysterious disappearance of Professor Victor Bergman from the last series of the Gerry Anderson TV series (for which Ball had earlier authored *The Space Guardians* in 1975). *Survival* was published in the U.S. by Powys Media in 2005. Its quality was such that Ball was quickly commissioned to write a new *Space: 1999* novelette for the same publisher, intended for a new *Space: 1999* anthology, *Shepherd Moon*. Unfortunately, this book and his story "Cargo" has yet to appear.

Following the publication of *Survival*, Ball was assigned to write a new *UFO* novel (based on another iconic Gerry Anderson TV series) by the UK publisher, Fanderson. Unfortunately, his superb novel *The Dark Time* is still in limbo, following the suspension of Fanderson's TV tie-in books programme. Happily, his next new novel, a supernatural thriller, *did* appear. *Malice of the Soul* was published in the UK in 2008, and is also scheduled to appear soon from the Borgo Press.

TIME FOR MURDER

When Chalmers decides to attend one of Dr. Lanson's nightly séances, it's not because he has any belief in the occult, but simply to find somewhere warm to rest his weary feet. It's a decision he soon regrets. First, a luminous cloud forms in the air over the heads of the assembled people. A strange voice speaks, warning that someone in the room is about to die to prevent him from revealing secrets. The man sitting next to him leaps to his feet, yelling his defiance—and then the lights are extinguished. As the man's voice is cut off, a girl's ear-piercing shriek reverberates...and Terror Stalks the Séance Room!

Just one of eleven exciting macabre crime short stories by a master of the form!

Borgo Press Books by SYDNEY J. BOUNDS

Boomerang: A Crime Novel
Time for Murder: Macabre Crime Stories
The World Wrecker: A Science Fiction Novel

TIME FOR MURDER

MACABRE CRIME STORIES

SYDNEY J. BOUNDS

Edited by Philip Harbottle

THE BORGO PRESS

MMXII

TIME FOR MURDER

FIRST BORGO PRESS EDITION

Published by Wildside Press LLC

www.wildsidebooks.com

DEDICATION

For Maureen Shine

CONTENTS

ACKNOWLEDGMENTS

These stories were previously published individually as follows, and are reprinted by permission of the author's Estate and his agent, Cosmos Literary Agency:

"Time for Murder" was originally published in *Authentic Science Fiction*, October, 1955. Copyright © 1955 by Sydney J. Bounds.

"Terror in the Séance Room" was first published in *Suspense Stories* #2, September 1954. Copyright © 1954 by Sydney J. Bounds.

"The House in the Pines" appears here for the first time. Copyright © 2012 by the Estate of Sydney J. Bounds.

"The Organ Bank Caper" was originally published in *Mystique: Tales of Wonder*, January 1988. Copyright © 1988 by Sydney J. Bounds.

"The Crime at Black Dyke" appears here for the first time. Copyright © 2012 by the Estate of Sydney J. Bounds.

"The Book Miser" was originally published in *Whodunit? The First Borgo Press Book of Crime and Mystery Stories*, edited by Robert Reginald, Borgo Press, 2011. Copyright © 2011 by the Estate of Sydney J. Bounds.

"The Footprints" was originally published in *The First UK Paperback and Pulp Bookfair Official Souvenir Booklet*. September 1991. Copyright © 1991 by Sydney J. Bounds.

"Downmarket" was originally published in *The Mammoth Book of Monsters*. Copyright © 2007 by the Estate of Sydney

TIME FOR MURDER

The corpse was dressed in a well-cut suit of black pinstripe, with white shirt, stiff collar, and black bow tie. It lay across a Persian rug with the pointed toes of patent leather shoes aimed at the ceiling. A neat round hole, rust-brown at the edges, spoilt the freshly laundered shirt.

Inspector Burton listened attentively while the local constable read aloud from his notebook:

"Gerald Laver, age sixty-three, financier, bachelor, lived alone except for one servant. Shot through the heart from a distance of three yards by a .45 automatic—that's the gun on the table—died instantly. Time of death established by medical evidence, nine to nine-thirty p.m. Wrist watch smashed and stopped at nine twenty-one p.m."

Burton glanced at his own watch. It was ten thirty-two. "An hour ago. How did you get here so fast?"

"Tip-off by phone—anonymous, of course."

"The servant?"

"No. He was at the cinema—arrived back at ten-three. We were here before that."

Burton's gaze shifted from the two C.I.D. men taking measurements to the gun lying on the table top.

"Any prints?"

"Yes, good and clear—he'll swing for this."

"Motive?"

"Established—this case is so easy, a recruit out of Hendon could wrap it up! Papers in the desk show that Clifford Webb,

a research physicist, was heavily in debt to Laver, that tonight repayment fell due. With Laver dead, he doesn't have to pay a penny."

"Sounds too easy. Where's the catch?"

The constable shook his head. "No catch."

"All right," Burton said. "Let's pick up Webb."

* * * * * * *

They picked up Webb. The prints on the gun were his. The serial number proved he had bought the gun only a week before. He admitted that he was in debt to Laver.

Clifford Webb was arrested, charged with the murder of Gerald Laver and brought to trial.

He pleaded not guilty and, when the question of timing was brought out, caused a sensation by proving conclusively that he was nowhere near Laver's house at nine twenty-one on the night of the murder.

As a member of the Royal Society, he had arrived at Burlington House at ten minutes to eight, listened with a hundred other members to Professor Smythe's paper—then, at eight forty-five, commenced reading his own paper on *Thermodynamics for a Space-Time Continuum.* He finished reading the paper at nine thirty-five, answered a number of questions, and left Burlington House shortly after ten o'clock. With more than a hundred witnesses, his alibi could not be broken.

Clifford Webb was acquitted of a charge of murder.

* * * * * * *

Inspector Burton stared glumly at his desk and wondered how the gun that had killed Laver could clearly show Webb's fingerprints, and no others, if Webb had not been the last man to handle it. He already had a headache from thinking about that.

His sergeant brought him a mug of sweetened tea. "Tough time with the commissioner, inspector?"

"The old man damn near read me the book. It's a perishing wonder I'm not pounding a beat again!"

The sergeant clucked like a sympathetic hen. "Odd sort of case, inspector. If it weren't for that alibi—"

Burton spluttered and slammed down his mug of tea. It slopped over the desk, ruining a report he was working on. "Don't mention alibis to me!"

The sergeant offered his cigarettes. Burton took one, flicked the wheel of his lighter, and inhaled gratefully. The sergeant waited a few seconds, then said, hesitantly: "There was another odd thing I noticed—"

He paused.

"Yes?" prompted the inspector.

"I didn't mention it before because it seemed crazy—it still does, but maybe you ought to know about it. After you'd left Laver's house, I was alone with the corpse, waiting for the mortuary van to come. It was quiet in that room. Just me and the deceased—then, all at once, there was this rabbit."

"Rabbit! What rabbit?" Burton stared at the sergeant. "Did you say, rabbit?" he repeated.

"That's right, sir—a fluffy white rabbit with pink eyes and long ears. It was running round the room, then, suddenly—it wasn't there anymore. Vanished right under my nose!"

Burton looked at his sergeant long and hard. "Drinking intoxicating liquor on duty?" he suggested.

"No, sir, hadn't touched a drop."

Burton thought of the fingerprints on Webb's automatic...and now a white rabbit!

"You're not suggesting it was the rabbit who shot Gerald Laver?"

"Of course not, sir. But it does seem odd, that rabbit coming from nowhere and then disappearing. I just thought I'd mention it."

Burton stubbed out his cigarette, taking his time about it, but before he could think of an adequate reply, the telephone rang. He picked up the receiver. "Yes...speaking. Who? I see.... I'll

come over right away. Goodbye."

He cradled the phone thoughtfully, turning to the sergeant. "Guess who?" he invited.

"The commissioner?"

Burton glared. "You've a lousy sense of humour. No, that was Clifford Webb, and he wants me to call on him."

"Perhaps he wants to confess?" the sergeant suggested.

* * * * * *

Clifford Webb was a head taller than Burton, a rangy man with a sharply-pointed nose and eyes that never quite seemed to focus in one place. He was wearing a white laboratory coat as he greeted the inspector.

"Nice of you to spare the time, inspector. Can I offer you a drink?"

"Thanks, no."

Webb grinned sardonically.

"Could be you object to drinking with a murderer!"

Burton refused to be drawn. Looking round the comfortably furnished room, he asked: "What did you want to see me about?"

Webb waved him to a chair, then moved across to the fireplace. His eyes focused briefly on Burton's face.

"As I understand the law," he said, "now that I have been acquitted of Laver's murder, I cannot again be charged with that crime. Correct?"

Burton nodded.

"Good! Now, inspector, prepare yourself for a shock. I did kill Gerald Laver—and I'll tell you how."

Burton took a cigarette from his case and lit it. "Just why are you telling me this?" he asked, bluntly.

"Vanity, inspector, pure vanity. I have committed the perfect crime. Naturally, I want you to know—now that you can't do a damn thing about it! I thought you might have guessed from the title of the paper I read to the Royal Society. Remember? It was

called *Thermodynamics for a Space-Time Continuum*. Time, inspector, that's the clue you missed....

"Time is an imperfectly understood medium. Perhaps dimension would be a better word. The fourth dimension, it is usually called. An object can have its position in space fixed by the dimensions of length, breadth, and depth—but unless we say that it exists in this space for a certain *time*, how can we say that its position is fixed at all?"

Burton declined to answer.

"I have long desired to experiment with the dimension of time, to travel through the fourth dimension as we now travel through space, and it was Laver who gave me the opportunity. He advanced the money for my experiments. He wanted a machine that would travel into the past, thinking by this means to cheat death and attain immortality! He did not realise that such a transference would automatically set up a new future for himself, involving a new death.

"For myself, I was interested in the practical applications for crime. Not that I have any interest in crime, as such, but scientific research costs money, and I saw the chance of getting that money. For instance, I could retreat into the past, commit a robbery, then return to the present and fix an unbreakable alibi. Interested, inspector?"

Burton nodded, shredding the end of his cigarette with his teeth.

"I succeeded," Clifford Webb continued. "I built my machine, and now, if you will follow us, I'll show it to you. But don't expect anything spectacular—this isn't Hollywood."

Burton followed the physicist through a door and along a passage to the laboratory. In the centre of the room, he saw a doorframe surrounded by the coils of wire helices. A control panel was marked off in an elaborate time-scale.

"Doesn't look much, does it, inspector? But I can assure you it works."

Burton looked at Webb, and knew that if he wasn't dealing with a madman then he was with a murderer.

"How?" he grunted.

"The maths involved are of a very high order," Webb said, "so you must be content with analogies. When I pass an electric current through my helices, a field of energy is created which distorts the space-time continuum. Space as well as time, you will note. In effect, I can step through my door frame into another time and arrive at a different location from this room!

"I still don't see how you faked your alibi," Burton grunted.

"But it's so simple, inspector. I had already decided to kill Laver—he was threatening to foreclose on his loan. I attended the Royal Society, arriving back here about half-past ten. I adjusted the time-scale of my machine to nine-twenty, the space location to Laver's study. Then I stepped through."

Webb's eyes glittered, his breath quickened.

"As I expected, I was in Gerald Laver's study—and he was taken completely by surprise. I shot him, phoned the police, and returned here. I had only to wait for you to prove my alibi!"

"I still don't see how you could be in two places at once," Burton said.

"How can I explain it? Time is not like a river flowing in one direction. Think of it as a tapestry; the flow of time corresponds to the warp, the lengthwise threads—but there is also the woof, the crosswise threads. These represent our position in the time-stream—and note please that the warp has *infinite* threads. Perhaps you can imagine it as a series of parallel worlds; we have a possible existence in each, but are only aware of one! I killed Laver in another world, on a different warp of the tapestry...things might have gone wrong, I admit. When I returned, Laver might not have died in this world. My interference with time could have upset my alibi. Perhaps I would have been stranded in that space-time where I killed Laver. Anything might have happened, but I was lucky and it worked out the way I planned."

Burton threw away the butt of his cigarette. "And now that you've been acquitted, you are perfectly safe," he said, slowly. "Yes, you're right—it is a perfect crime."

Webb smiled complacently.

"Perhaps you'd like to see a demonstration, inspector?"

Burton nodded, and the physicist switched on the power and made an adjustment to the time-scale. The helices began to glow and, between the limits of the doorframe, appeared a blackness so intense that the Inspector could not bear to look into it.

Webb removed a white rabbit from a hutch on his work bench.

"Daisy," he said, smoothing back the rabbit's long ears, "is the world's most experienced time-traveller. I've used her for many experiments and she has always returned unharmed. I doubt if she knows what a remarkable rabbit she is!"

Burton stared, remembering his sergeant's story. The hairs at the nape of his neck began to bristle.

"I am sending her back to a period a little after the time of the murder," Webb said, "the location as before—Laver's study. Perhaps one of your men reported seeing Daisy? In which case, we mustn't disappoint him...." He set Daisy on the floor before the door into time and gently urged her through it. Instantly, she vanished from view.

Burton walked warily round the door in the centre of the room. He completed a full circuit without seeing anything of Daisy.

"Convinced, inspector? She will appear again in one minute—I have set the automatic control for that period."

The seconds ticked by. Burton studied the time-scale carefully; a plan was shaping in his head, a plan to bring Clifford Webb to justice.

"Here she is, inspector!" the physicist exclaimed triumphantly.

He lifted the rabbit from the floor and placed her back inside her hutch.

Burton moved silently and, as Webb turned from the hutch, swung his fist to the physicist's jaw. Webb slumped unconscious to the floor.

Burton studied the controlling mechanism of the time machine yet again. It seemed simple enough. He adjusted the

time-scale for nine-twenty of the night of the murder. Webb had already told him that the space location was Laver's study. He had only to step through to catch the murderer red-handed.

He took one last look at the unconscious form of Clifford Webb and stepped between the glowing helices into blackness....

There was the Persian rug, but Laver was not now stretched out upon it. The financier faced Clifford Webb, staring fascinated at the gun in his hand. Webb's finger tightened on the trigger.

"Stop!"

The command was torn from Burton's lips as if of its own volition. Webb half-turned, amazement written plain across his face—and, in that moment of hesitation, Laver hurled himself across the room to grapple with his would-be murderer.

Burton heard the shot, and saw one of the two men stagger and fall across the Persian rug. He looked down.

The corpse had been a rangy man with a sharply pointed nose. The eyes, which in life had never quite seemed to focus in one place, were now focused in death on the ceiling. Clifford Webb had paid in full for his intended crime.

"It was self-defence!" Gerald Laver screamed. "You saw it— he threatened me—I killed him in self-defence!"

Inspector Burton scratched his head and wondered what the commissioner would make of his report.

TERROR STALKS
THE SÉANCE ROOM

CHAPTER 1: DR. LANDON—MEDIUM

It was one of those nights when even a cadaver feels chilled to the bone. A raw-cold mist swirled in from the sea, swallowing Manhattan Island in a grey shroud.

Down on the East Side, Burt Chambers shrugged a thin jacket tighter about his broad shoulders. There were fifty cents in his pocket, a lethargy in the way he dragged his huge body along the sidewalk, and no hope in his heart.

The dismal wail of a tug's hooter echoed through the mist, reminding him of the nearness of the Hudson River. The Hudson, with its ice-cold waters, bleak and comfortless—but so final. How many derelicts of Life's relentless progress had ended up in those black waters?

You either went on—or under. Life—or Death. It was so easy, so tempting. You let the icy chill freeze your body, let the dank waters slide smoothly over your head. Then it was all over. No more fighting, no more living—no more loving. Abruptly, Burt Chalmers pushed the idea out of his head. He shuddered and turned away.

A red light winked at him through the greyness. A building loomed ahead. He followed the brownstone wall till he came to the doorway. Over the porch, a red neon sign flickered luridly. He stopped to read the sign.

DR. LANSON—MEDIUM
Séances nightly—all welcome.

Chalmers laughed wolfishly. Just another racket to clean out the suckers. Mumbo-jumbo and stage magic—and Dr. Lanson raked in the greenbacks.

He was about to pass on when the idea struck him. Why not take advantage of Dr. Lanson's hospitality? All welcome, the sign said. And he was cold and footsore—past caring where his next meal or the night's lodging came from.

He stared blindly into the damp mist eddying around the house. He heard a car go past, but the mist was now so thick he couldn't even make out the highlights. He shivered, looked in at the open doorway—at least it would be warm in there. And he could take the weight off his feet.

There were two steps up to the porch. Then a short passage and a flight of wooden stairs. There was no carpet on the stairs and his heavy feet echoed eerily on the bare boards. At the top of the stairs a closed door bore the notice:

Please. Walk in.

"Said the Spider to the Fly!" he murmured, pushing open the door.

His first impression was that he had wandered on to the set of a Hollywood epic—Oriental style.

The floor was thickly carpeted, the walls hung with bizarre tapestries. There was a half-circle of chairs, about two-thirds of them filled with people. Chalmers sank easily into the nearest that was empty.

In the centre, a thin-faced man with a pointed beard and pince-nez was mumbling an incantation over a brazier. The brazier glowed redly, the only illumination in the room. Incense burned in bronze chalices, filling the room with a pungent sweetness.

Chalmers dozed. The room was warm, the air heavy with the

sickly incense. He nodded—caught himself as he almost rolled off the chair. He looked around, studying the faces of the people intent on the man over the brazier.

A mixed lot. One white-haired lady from the West Side, over-burdened with jewellery. A lamb to the slaughter. A middle-class wife who had dragged along her bored husband. Wrinkled faces, bright eyes in dead faces, the faces of people living on after life had gone. Waiting the call from beyond the grave.

Chalmers felt sorry for them. At least he hadn't reached that stage yet. Then he saw the girl. He straightened in his seat to get a better look at her.

She was young. Nineteen, maybe twenty. And beautiful. Her figure was the sort you pay big money on Broadway—just to look at. She had black hair, falling down over smooth shoulders. The dark oval of her face was tinted redly by the glowing coals in the brazier. Wide, dark eyes watched the man performing the incantation.

When she looked up, Chalmers saw that the pupils of her eyes were dilated with fear. Her lips moved soundlessly. Her fingers beat an uneasy tattoo on her knee. Her fear communicated itself to him. He shivered and looked away. What was the girl afraid of?

He watched her out of the corner of his eye. Her hand strayed to the man next to her. She gripped his wrist till it gleamed whitely in the firelight. Chalmers saw him glance at her, pat her hand as if to reassure her.

Chalmers wished it were he doing the reassuring. She was sure a cute number, Then he remembered Joyce—

He scowled and looked away. But the feeling persisted. This beautiful young girl was frightened—badly frightened. And Chalmers wanted to do something about it.

He wondered who the man was sitting next to her. He studied him carefully. A thin man, well-dressed, with a pale face and blue eyes. He wondered if the man were her fiancé. A glance at the engagement ring on the girl's finger confirmed this possi-bility. But what was either of them doing at this pseudo-fetish?

The man, Chalmers saw, was all tensed up. Not frightened like the girl, but taut. Taut as a bowstring. His face showed plainly that he was waiting for something to happen. What was he waiting for? The same thing that frightened the girl?

Chalmers let his eyes wander to the man by the brazier. Dr. Lanson? A long robe, decorated with crescents and interlocked triangles, dropped to his ankles. His feet were covered by thin moccasins, his head by a turban from which a large ruby glittered.

As he chanted sibilant runes, Dr. Lanson's slim white fingers cast a powder onto the glowing coals. The powder burnt blood-red, filling the room with the overpowering smell of a musky perfume. The atmosphere thickened. Chalmers felt his breath catch on the pungent empyreuma.

Dr. Lanson's assistant stood in the shadows behind him. Chalmers hadn't noticed him before, so still and silent was he. A small man with a red, wrinkled face and gnarled hands. The right hand twitched and Chalmers saw that the small finger was missing.

Three Fingers wore a chocolate coat with a chocolate tie against a white shirt. His shoes were white with chocolate-brown toe-caps. A cloth cap was pulled down over his forehead so that his eyes were covered.

Chalmers' attention was suddenly jerked back to Dr. Lanson. The medium had ceased his incantation. Now he stood upright, arms outstretched above his head. Bright, piercing eyes glittered behind the pince-nez, and his short, pointed beard jutted out like the finger of an avenging devil. He spoke in a loud, clear voice that carried to every corner of the room.

"Ai! Ai! In the name of the Horned One, the Shadow that blots out all Light, the Toad spawning in the darkness beyond the Universe, 1 command thee—Belchior, spirit messenger from the Other life beyond the veil of Death—come forth!"

In the moment of awful silence that followed Dr. Lanson's pronouncement, Chalmers felt his body go rigid. The hairs on the nape of his neck stiffened. Sweat broke out on his forehead.

He forced himself to relax. Mumbo-jumbo and stage magic. Nothing to it. It was the setting, the red glow of coals in the brazier, the thick carpets and curtains, the sickly smell of incense that got him. Nothing else.

He glanced at the other people in the room. Without exception, they strained forward in their seats, expectantly, hopefully. The girl's face was white. A tiny trickle of blood oozed down her chin as she bit her lip. The man beside her seemed to be in a trance—his face ashen....

Chalmers started. A luminous cloud formed in the air over the heads of the assembled people. It swirled mistily, an eerie blue light emanating from the centre of the cloud. Chalmers' lip curled. How could anyone be taken in so easily? A luminous gas released from a vent in the wall.

A voice spoke out of the cloud. A curiously flat voice, as if it had travelled a long way and lost its resonance on the journey. Ventriloquism. Chalmers watched Three Fingers to see if he could detect the assistant's mouth moving. But Three Fingers was too far back, too much in the shadow to tell.

The flat voice from the cloud said:

"I am here, O Master. What is your wish?"

Dr. Lanson's clear tones rang through the room.

"There are those here who would speak with one who has passed the barrier. Is there one to answer?"

The silence that came was almost tangible. It was heavy, oppressive. It seemed that everyone had stopped breathing. Chalmers forced himself to expel the air from his lungs. The sound was like a balloon deflating.

The voice from the eerie blue cloud came again:

"There is one here who would speak with someone on the other side—"

The gathering craned forward. White faces gleamed in the red light of the coals. Chalmers felt himself carried with them. He, too, felt the wave of tension surge through the room. The voice might be a trick—he told himself it must be a trick—but in that incense-perfumed murk it was strangely convincing.

A second voice strained through the luminous cloud, It was high-pitched, with an odd rhythm to it—a sing-song chanting that seemed to race ahead of the words. Chalmers watched Three Fingers' face, but his lips were in shadow. It was impossible to tell if he was the owner of the voice.

"I speak to one in the room on the other side," chanted the sing-song voice. "It is a man. He is in great danger. The scythe of the Grim Reaper swings above his head. The Sands of Time run low. I see the bony skull of Death grinning over his shoulder—"

A coldness seemed to seep into the room. A shudder ran through the crowd. Chalmers felt his flesh crawl. The high-pitched voice sang on:

"A warning to this man. Let him heed the voices of his advisers. Silence is demanded if he is to avert the threat hanging over him. Silence. A man with secrets needs be a man without a tongue—"

Too many things happened in a hurry for Chalmers ever to sort out their order of occurrence.

As the chanting died away, the eerie cloud seemed to lose its luminosity and disperse. The man with the pale face and blue eyes, next to the girl, leapt to his feet.

"You can't frighten me!" he cried, half-sobbing. "I know your game—I won't keep quiet—"

Chalmers' eyes flicked from the dead-white face of the girl to Dr. Lanson. The medium's hands hovered over the brazier. A fine powder dropped from his sleeves onto the glowing coals. Abruptly, the coals spluttered and went out, plunging the room into darkness.

The man's voice was cut off.

Chalmers froze in his seat as the girl's ear-piercing shriek reverberated through the room.

CHAPTER 2: THE LADY IS FRIGHTENED

Burt Chalmers came out of his seat like a shot from a catapult. He rocketed across the room in the direction of the girl, knocking chairs flying in the dark. He heard a grunt as he collided with someone, staggered, and lost his sense of direction.

He lost seconds fumbling in his pocket for a match, struck it impatiently. The yellow flare revealed the girl's taut figure. She was standing upright, rigid, one hand over her mouth to choke the scream swelling in her throat.

He dropped a hand on her shoulder.

"What—?" he began.

Her painted nails clawed at his face She made a strange noise, half scream, half sob. She turned, struck at Chalmers again, and fled across the room to the door.

He staggered back under her blow. Scared as Hell, he thought. What had frightened her in the dark? He wiped his stinging face where her hand had struck him. His hand came away wet. He rubbed his fingers together, smelt them. Blood! His face wasn't cut—so it must have come from her hand as she hit him.

The girl had reached the door and jerked it open. The lamp in the hall at the top of the stairs shone faint beams into the room. Chalmers glimpsed the startled people milling around him. Dr. Lanson was still standing over the brazier, but of Three Fingers there was no sign.

Suddenly he remembered the man who had been with the girl—the man who had been warned by the phoney voice from the grave. Where was he? Chalmers was prepared to swear that no one except the girl had left through the door. His eyes swept round the room without alighting on the man he sought.

He caught sight of some red spots on the carpet, between the chairs where the girl and her fiancé had been sitting. He knelt down and smeared the spots with his fingers. Blood!

Chalmers rose to his feet. His lips set in a grim line. Murder! But the corpse has disappeared—and so had Three Fingers.

And the girl was scared and running wild in New York's East Side. If Chalmer's suspicions were correct, she was in grave danger.

Ignoring the chatter of the people around him, Chalmers crossed to the door and clattered noisily down the stairs after the girl.

The red neon sign still invited all to the nightly séance held by Dr. Lanson, and the mist still swirled greyly about the brownstone house. He paused on the steps, trying to decide which way she had gone. He strained his ears, heard the faint clicking of high heels on the sidewalk, and hurried off towards the sound.

He ran fast, letting his long legs carry his bulk in easy, loping strides. The mist thinned a little at the end of the block, and he caught a glimpse of the girl as she darted across the road under the yellow light of a street-lamp.

She looked round, her face white, and started running again. Hell, Chalmers thought, she's heard me—and thinks I'm one of the gang after her. He lengthened his stride, quickened his pace.

He caught her at the next intersection. She was out of breath and leaning heavily against the street-lamp. Chalmers put his arms round her to keep her hands out of his face.

"Now take it easy, lady," he said smoothly. "I'm not going to hurt you. 1 guess you're in bad trouble, and if there's anything I can do to help, you've only to say so. At least, allow me to escort you home."

Her reaction caught him unawares. She flung her arms round his neck, buried her face in his chest, and burst into tears

"They murdered him!" she sobbed. "They'll kill me next— oh, don't let them get me—save me—please...."

Chalmers soothed her gently. Poor kid, she'd had a tough time. Scared out of her wits. Living on her nerve and now it was gone. His rough hands caressed her.

"Now don't worry," he said quietly. "No one's going to hurt you while Burt Chalmers is around. Dry your eyes and I'll see you safely home."

She lifted her face to him and tried to smile.

"Thank you," she said. "I'll be all right now."

Chalmers looked down at her. His mouth went dry and he felt his pulse quicken as he held her close. God, she was beautiful!

The yellow street-light showed high cheek-bones and wide, appealing eyes. Her lips were full and very red. He wanted to crush his mouth over hers....

She was wearing a dark-red dress that moulded itself to her young curves. Her legs were long and slim and encased in sheer silk hose.

Chalmers pushed her away from him.

"Where to?" he asked abruptly.

She gave an address a dozen blocks away, and Burt put his arm around her slim waist and piloted her through the mist. She didn't speak on the way to her home and he respected her silence. When they arrived at the apartment house where she lived, she invited him inside.

"A drink?" she suggested.

Chalmers said, laconically: "Beer."

She smiled faintly.

"There's only brandy, I'm afraid."

He nodded briefly.

"Please sit down," she said, indicating the straight-backed sofa along one wall.

Chalmers sat down. The girl poured two brandies, passed him one, and sat down beside him. She emptied her glass in one gulp and refilled it. Chalmers sipped his slowly, letting the fiery liquid roll around his tongue, warming him.

He was aware that her eyes were on him, puzzling over his derelict appearance, wondering how far she could trust him.

Chalmers smoothed his blond hair back with a broad hand, ran his fingers round the stubble of his chin. He wished he had shaved that morning.

"You look like a down and out," she said critically, "but then again—you don't, if you get what I mean."

Chalmers drained the brandy from his glass and turned grey eyes on her. He waved a large hand casually.

"It's not a new story," he said. His smile was bitter. "I was in the U.S. Marines—sergeant—and I fell for a good-looking dame. Fell like a log. I worshipped the very ground she walked on. Nothing was too good for her."

He fell silent, reliving the past. Quietly, the girl refilled his glass. He sipped appreciatively and went on:

"We were married and I got my discharge. We were going to buy a little place in the country—up in Maine—and settle down to raise a family. I was held up by a lot of red tape and she persuaded me to make all my savings over to her so she could go right ahead and fix things up for when I got out. It was one swell idea—for her! Of course, I didn't see her again—nor my money. I was just another sucker taken for a ride. So I ended up flat broke, out of a job, and out of the Marines. To make everything perfect, I found out she already had a husband—so I wasn't even married!"

The girl's dark eyes were soft and pitying.

"That's a bad deal. I figure a guy like you deserves something better than a runaround. What's your name again?"

"Chalmers. My friends call me Burt."

"I'm Ann, Burt. Ann Stevens. I'm in terrible trouble. I think they're going to murder me."

Burt took her hand in his.

"No one's going to murder you if I can stop them," he said softly. "Suppose you tell me what it's all about?"

Ann looked at him in silence. Her raven-black hair fell down over slim shoulders and Chalmers caught a whiff of exotic perfume. He had to fight to control himself. He wanted to grab her and kiss her—but he knew if he tried anything like that with this girl, everything would be over between them. And he wanted their friendship to develop.

At last, she made up her mind.

"I believe I can trust you, Burt," she said, "and God knows, I need someone I can trust. It's not such a simple story as yours, and I don't have all the pieces of the puzzle yet. I only know that Dudley was murdered in that horrible room back there—and

I'm in terrible danger."

She pulled out a cigarette case and offered it to Burt. He took one and lit it gratefully. It tasted good—he hadn't smoked in three days.

"Dudley was the man you were with at the séance?" he queried. "'Your fiancé?"

Ann nodded, drawing on her cigarette and blowing a smoke ring. She watched the ring rise slowly to the ceiling.

"Yes," she agreed, "Dudley Brooks and I were engaged to be married. The wedding was to have been next month."

Burt said, trying hard to sound as if he meant it:

"I'm sorry."

Ann shrugged.

"It's all over now," she said fatalistically. Her voice was perfectly calm. "It was through Dudley that I first met Dr. Lanson and the people who go to his séances."

She shuddered and inhaled deeply on the cigarette.

"I had known Dudley all my life. We went to the same school and grew up together. It was tacitly assumed by our families that eventually we would marry—but I never really loved him."

Burt felt a lot better hearing that. He didn't like the idea of stealing a dead man's love. But that confession made it all right.

"Dudley was very interested in the occult. I suppose you'd call him a student of the occult. He used to go to séances and investigate different forms of black magic. He has a library at home filled with all kinds of books dealing with sorcery and the Black Arts."

"You mean he took that kind of thing seriously?" Chalmers interrupted, a look of incredulous wonder on his rugged face. "It stuck out a mile back there that Dr. Lanson was a phoney. A cloud of gas and a ventriloquist throwing his voice and all the old dames lapping up the message from the other side!"

"Oh, Dudley knew there was a lot of faking connected with mediums and their powers, but he believed that one or two of them really did have some strange power that other people haven't got. And it was in hope of contacting the few genuine

mediums that he investigated every séance he could."

Ann paused to stub out her cigarette in the china ashtray on the small table beside the sofa.

"Another brandy?" she suggested.

Burt shook his head.

"Not for me—I know when to stop.'"

She smiled and continued her story:

"When Dudley first met Dr. Lanson, he was quite sure he was a fake—but he couldn't prove it. So he went to his séances regularly in the hope of getting proof. Well, one day he found out that the séances were only a blind for a bigger racket. He was very worried about this, but wouldn't tell me what he had learnt. I know he was scared about it and considered that Dr. Lanson should be exposed, and he tried to make me keep out of it. But I couldn't let him face whatever it was alone, so I went with him as often as I could."

"Did you get any kind of line on what it was he discovered?" Chalmers asked.

Ann hesitated, then shook her head.

"No—except that it concerned what Dudley called Dr. Lanson's Inner Circle. I got the impression they meet once a month—but not at the place we were at tonight. I don't know where."

Chalmers considered what Ann had told him.

"It boils down to this, then. Dudley found out something about Dr. Lanson that automatically made him a candidate for a coffin—and because you've been around with him, you're in danger of the same treatment. You could go to the police—but your story's too thin for official recognition. Dudley disappeared—we can't produce the body. You can bet Dr. Lanson has cleaned the bloodstains off the carpet by now. I can corroborate your statement but it's hardly likely the police will take any notice of an out-of-work bum. Meanwhile, you're liable to turn up in the Hudson with your throat cut."

Ann shuddered.

"What am I going to do?" she asked.

Chalmers' grey eyes regarded her levelly.

"If you feel you can trust me, Ann," he said, "I'd like to stick around and look after you."

She gave him her hand. Chalmers pressed it warmly.

"I do trust you, Burt—and I'd really like to have you around."

"That's a deal," he said.

"It's late now," Ann said, "what are you going to do? Will you stop here?"

She blushed as she realised what she had said.

"I mean," she ran on hurriedly, "you can sleep on the couch here."

Chalmers grinned,

"That'll do me."

Ann quickly made up a bed on the couch.

"I'll sleep easier knowing you're out here," she said.

She looked at him from lowered eyelashes. Her lips parted in a smile—then she skipped across the room and kissed him lightly on the mouth.

"Good night, Burt," she said softly, and turned and ducked into the bedroom.

Chalmers stood motionless, staring after her slim young figure. He grinned. Then the key turned in the lock and he was alone in the room.

CHAPTER 3: THREE FINGERS AGAIN

Chalmers lay on the couch in the dark. He listened to the loud ticking of the clock over the mantelpiece and the light breathing of the girl in the room next door.

The clock struck twice. Two a.m. Chalmers shifted the pillow under his head and turned over. His grey eyes were wide and he had never felt less sleepy in his life.

He rubbed thoughtfully at the stubble of blond hair coating his jaw and wondered if he was making a fool of himself again. When he remembered Joyce, the curvaceous armful who had

skipped with his savings, he felt a bitter distrust of all females.

And here he was, playing knight in armour to Ann's damsel in distress. A smile flickered briefly about his lips and went out. The stakes were higher this time. If he lost out now, he'd end up with the worms in the graveyard.

He considered the idea of getting to his feet and walking out. He owed the girl nothing—why should he stick his neck out for her? But the more he thought about her, the more certain he became that he'd never leave her to the mercy of Dr. Lanson and his killers.

The taste of her goodnight kiss still lingered about his lips— and it was a flavour he wanted to experience again. And her dark eyes had held the promise of more intimate favours to come if he got her out of this jam....

A soft click at the door alerted him. He rolled off the couch and dropped softly on the balls of his stockinged feet. The noise was repeated some minutes later. Chalmers crouched down behind the sofa, straining his eyes in the dark, watching the door.

He guessed that someone was trying to pick the lock. There was a gentle thud as the key was pushed out of the lock to drop on the mat inside. Then. a louder click as the tumblers snapped back. The door opened quietly and a black shadow glided into the room.

A torch beam flicked round the room. Chalmers ducked hastily as the beam of light played over the couch—but the glimpse he'd had was sufficient to identify the intruder. It was Three Fingers, Dr. Lanson's assistant.

The torchlight snapped off and Three Fingers moved silently towards the door of Ann's bedroom. Chalmers let him go to work on the lock before he moved, then he stepped from cover and crept up on him.

His intention had been to take his quarry from behind, banking on the element of surprise to offset the advantage of any weapon the other might have. But his luck was out. Even as Chalmers tensed himself to grapple with his opponent, Three

Fingers, alarmed by some slight sound, turned sideways.

Chalmers' hands, which should have gone round Three Fingers' throat, thudded harmlessly against the man's body as he straightened up.

Snarling, Three Fingers dropped his torch and snatched out a glittering ice pick. Chalmers dropped flat as the point of the ice pick buried itself in the woodwork over his head. He didn't need telling how Dudley Brooks had been silenced so efficiently at the séance.

Three Fingers followed up his attack by flinging himself at Chalmers, wrapping his arms about him. Chalmers threw himself backwards onto the floor, carrying Three Fingers with him and breaking his hold.

Despite his extra height and weight, Chalmers found his opponent a slippery customer. The smaller man wriggled like an eel, twisting and lunging viciously with his fists. They rolled across the room, locked in a deadly embrace, each trying to finish the other in one swift, killing blow.

Chalmers got his hands round Three Fingers' throat. He started squeezing—staggered back with a cry of agony as he received a knee in the groin. He lay writhing on the floor, his eyes blinded by a flood of tears, while Three Fingers prepared to administer the death punch.

He heard a door open and the light clicked on. Ann Stevens, alarmed by the sound of fighting in the next room, had come out to see what was happening. Three Fingers turned his attention to her—unconsciously extending Chalmers' lease of life.

"Get away, Ann!" Chalmers croaked desperately. "Leave him to me!"

He climbed to his feet, ignoring the stabbing pain in his groin, and threw himself bodily at Three Fingers. He bore the killer to the floor and rolled atop him, slugging heavy punches to the smaller man's body.

Three Fingers wriggled clear—swung a short jab to Chalmers' solar plexus that stopped him cold. Chalmers swayed on his feet. Sweat ran down his face and into his mouth. It had

a salty tang.

He crouched low, covering his body with his arms as Three Fingers came in, swinging lefts and rights with telling force. He grabbed Three Fingers in a bear hug—his arms tightened. The air squeezed out of Three Fingers' lungs. Chalmers exerted all his force....

"Let him go," Ann's voice said from behind him, "I've got him covered."

Chalmers released the killer and stepped back. Too late he heard Ann say:

"It's a trick, Burt—watch out!"

As Three Fingers lunged forward, Chalmers saw that Ann was completely unarmed. In the brief span of time that it took the smaller man's arm to swing in a vicious arc, he remembered that Three Fingers was a ventriloquist—it had been Dr. Lanson's assistant, mimicking Ann's voice, who had spoken.

Chalmers realised that too late. It seemed as if a hand grenade exploded in his face. He felt himself falling—a dark pool opened up to engulf him—then nothingness....

* * * * * * *

A harsh light beat down into his eyes. His head throbbed like a power-crazy dynamo. His ears registered a confused blur of sound, which, as consciousness slowly returned, he identified as the jazzed-up pounding of his heart.

The floor beneath him was hard and unyielding. He tried to move his body—and his muscles shrieked agonizing protests. He let his mind sink back into semi-consciousness. The pain eased a little.

After a time he began to wonder who he was and where he was and how he had gotten into such a mess. He tried to solve the problem by thinking it out—but no solution came.

He decided it could be no more uncomfortable to stand up than it was to lie heaped-up on bone-bruising boards. Ignoring the pain, he lifted himself and clung to the mantelpiece.

A clock ticked ominously in his face. The hands stood at 2:25. He wondered whether it was a.m. or p.m. The glass over the mantelpiece showed a battered face, grey eyes, a stubble round the chin, and a tangle of blond hair. It looked familiar.

He licked his lips and tasted salt. His nose had been bleeding and the blood had run down into his mouth.

His first conscious memory was of Joyce. She must have hit him in the mouth with a flat-iron. But why should she do that? Hadn't she done enough to him already?

He was bitterly cursing all females when his eyes rested on the photograph of the girl with dark hair and deep black eyes. The photograph was standing in a metal frame on the mantelpiece beside the clock. And again the face seemed familiar. He read the name underneath: Ann Stevens.

And suddenly it all came back.

He remembered taking her home. And Three Fingers. There had been a fight. Then Ann came out of her bedroom—she had hastily thrown a dressing gown over silk pyjamas, but he still remembered admiring the perfection of her young figure before Three Fingers hit him for the last time.

Desperately, he called:

"Ann! Ann! Where are you, Ann?"

He searched the apartment, but he knew it was no good. Ann Stevens had disappeared. Fine watchdog you are, Burt Chalmers! What was he going to do now?

He looked at the clock, and this time it meant something. Half an hour had elapsed since Three Fingers had arrived, Time enough for him to get clean away—and there was no doubt that he had taken the girl with him.

The light was still on. He crossed to the window and peered out. The gray mist hung like a death shroud over Manhattan. No hope of tracing anyone in that.

Apparently, no one had been roused by the sound of the fight—or if they had, they had very prudently decided to mind their own business.

He searched the flat, pocketed some loose change Ann had

left on the table. The ice pick that had so nearly ended his career was still sticking in the door frame. He pulled it out and slipped it in his pocket. Quietly he left the apartment. Burt Chalmers badly wanted to meet Three Fingers again—there was something he had to settle with him....

CHAPTER 4: THE INNER CIRCLE

The police gave him a rough time. Of course, the Captain had eyed him with suspicion as soon as he entered the Homicide Bureau. His face was a mess, he hadn't shaved for three days, his coat was torn, and he looked like any other East Side bum.

The Captain listened to his story with the bored air of one who has heard it all before, Then he held him in the cooler while the night sergeant checked to see if the girl had disappeared. When he found out she had, the Captain gave him a going-over.

Finally, the police got around to Dr. Lanson's place. But the bare walls told them nothing. The doctor and his assistant had left in a hurry.

The Captain scratched his head and said it was up to the Missing Persons Bureau. Then they slung him out on the sidewalk because they couldn't cook up a charge to hold him any longer.

Burt Chalmers pounded East Side looking for Ann—or Dr. Lanson, or Three Fingers, or anyone who could give him a lead on the girl. Two days had passed since she had been taken from under his very nose. Two days which Chalmers had spent asking questions of the people neighbouring the house where the séances had been held; two days wearing out shoe-leather, hunting clues.

Maybe it had been a mistake to go to the police. If he hadn't wasted time, perhaps he could have picked up the trail while it was still warm. But he figured it was a police job—apparently the cops thought otherwise.

And, by now, Ann might be dead. His mouth tightened in a

thin line. If Dr. Lanson and Three Fingers had murdered her, he'd never rest until he'd evened the score. The ache in his heart told him how much the girl meant to him. He had to find her. But how?

He had exhausted all the possibilities he could think up. Dr. Lanson seemed to have disappeared into thin air—and New York was a big city to search. Assuming he was still in New York.

He turned into a drugstore for a coffee and sandwich. The sandwich was like sawdust in his mouth, the coffee tasteless. There was a paper lying on the tabletop. Idly he scanned the headlines to see if the police had discovered anything.

A murder at a nightspot. Baseball scores. Rioting in the South. He turned the pages disinterestedly, bitterly. What use paying a police force if they didn't do anything about Ann? The pages became a blur. He found the coffee had gone cold and he was down to the personal column. Two words caught his eye— *inner circle*.

Chalmers almost dropped the cup. The Inner Circle! That was the name Ann had given to the coterie on the inside of Dr. Lanson's racket. Eagerly, he read the notice:

The Inner Circle meets tonight at 11:30.

That was all. No name. No rendezvous.

He read it through three times, seeking for some hidden meaning. Did the notice concern Dr. Lanson, or was it merely the meeting of some quite innocuous society? Would the doctor have the nerve to insert a notice in the press, telling everyone who cared to read it when he was holding his next meeting?

Chalmers considered the point carefully. Why not? The notice wouldn't mean a thing to anyone not in the doctor's confidence. The more he thought about it, the more likely it seemed that it was a clue to Dr. Lanson—and through him, to Ann.

He lit a cigarette and tried to plan a course of action. It told him when the meeting was to be held, but not the more important factor—where. Of course. The members of the Inner Circle would know that. But Chalmers didn't.

A notice in the personal column. Someone would have to insert and pay for that. Who? Dr. Lanson? At least, someone in touch with him.

Chalmers shot across to the phone booth and jammed a nickel in the slot. He dialled the newspaper offices and got the department handling the personal ads.

A bored voice said:

"Can I help you?"

Chalmers poured syrup into his voice. He had to know the answer to his question.

"I'm ringing about an ad in today's paper," he said. "It gives the time of meeting of the Inner Circle, but unfortunately I've lost the address. If you could give me the address or the phone number of the person who inserted the ad, I could find out from them."

"Hold the line—I'll check back."

Chalmers waited in a sweat. It seemed a couple of weeks before the bored voice came back on the line.

"The ad was inserted by a Mr. Rivers. The address is 1116, East 47th Street. No phone number.'"

"Thanks—thanks a lot."

Chalmers jammed the receiver back on its rest with a sigh of relief. He had something to work on now. He ordered another coffee—it tasted like nectar this time—and sat down to plan his next step.

Call in the police? Not after the way they had treated him the last time. No, he'd handle this his own way. But, for Ann's sake, he couldn't afford to fail. He had no idea what sort of opposition he'd be up against. Dr. Lanson and Three Fingers, at least. And the mysterious Mr. Rivers. He needed a weapon. The police had taken the ice pick off him when they searched him at the station—a pity that—he'd dearly love to return that to Three Fingers.

A gun was the obvious thing. But he didn't possess one, and—even including the loose change he had picked up at Ann's flat—he didn't have the money to buy one. Then there was the

slight matter of a licence.

Well, there were other ways.

Chalmers got up and walked out of the drugstore. He walked around till he found a second-hand shop with a Colt .45 for sale. Then he walked around till closing time.

Five minutes before the shop was due to close, he walked in and up to the counter.

"Nice Colt you've got in the window," he said casually. "What's the price tag?"

The proprietor beamed at him.

"It's in good condition," he said, "nice action, cheap too— only twenty-five bucks. O.K.?"

"I'll take a closer look."

"Sure."

The proprietor hurried to the window, took the gun out of its case, and wiped the oil off it. He handed it to Chalmers for inspection.

Burt tried the action, lined up the sights. It was a nice job. Just what he wanted.

"Can you load it?"

"Sure—you gotta licence?"

"Yeah."

Chalmers took out his wallet and rifled through some papers, searching for an imaginary licence. The proprietor finished loading the chambers and put the gun down on the counter.

"I'll take a box of shells, too," Chalmers said.

The proprietor turned to get a box from the rack behind him. When he turned round again, he was facing a loaded Colt.

"No noise—no trouble!" Chalmers said grimly. He reached across, grabbed the box of shells, and stuck them in his pocket.

He yanked the telephone cable apart. He didn't want the cops on his trail as soon as he left the shop.

"You won't get far," the proprietor said.

"I'll take a chance. If you want to take a chance too—just stick your head out of the door and start yelling. I may be waiting around outside."

Keeping the shop proprietor covered, Chalmers backed over to the door. He ducked outside and started running, shoving the Colt out of sight in his pocket. He dived down the first subway entrance and took the first train out of the area. Then he doubled back and crossed his tracks.

He felt a lot better with the comforting bulge of a .45 in his pocket. Next stop 1116, East 47th, the Inner Circle and Dr. Lanson. Then Ann....

The residence of Mr. Rivers was a faded brick building with no pretence to cleanliness. It had a short flight of steps up to a wide porch. The door was solid with a heavy brass knocker.

Chalmers didn't use the knocker. He found himself a shadowy doorway opposite and settled down to wait.

It was just on eleven and a light in an upstairs window informed him that Mr. Rivers had not yet left for the meeting of the Inner Circle. The mist began to drift in from the sea. It swirled lazily round the doorway where Chalmers waited, hiding him from passing eyes.

A nearby clock struck eleven. As the last stroke reverberated on the clammy air, a cab drew up outside No. 1116. Chalmers tensed as the upstairs light blinked out. This was it. Rivers was about to leave for the meeting place.

He ducked across the road and spreadeagled himself across the luggage rack. He heard footsteps clatter down the stone steps, a mutter of voices, a door slam, then the cab moved off.

Cautiously Chalmers raised himself to look through the rear window. The shock of identifying the passenger almost caused him to lose his hold. The mysterious Mr. Rivers was none other than his old antagonist—Three Fingers!

Chalmers eased himself back onto the luggage rack. His breath came quicker. So his hunch had been right—and he was heading for Dr. Lanson's Inner Circle—and Ann.

The cab headed downtown. It was difficult to pick out the route in the grey mist, but the hooting of tugs told him they were near the river. The cab swung off the main thoroughfare and picked a devious route through twisting back streets.

As the clock struck the half-hour, the cab swung into the curb and stopped. Chalmers dropped off the rack and lost himself in the shadows. He saw Three Fingers get out and pay off the driver, then wait till the cab moved off out of sight.

Three Fingers waited a few minutes, then glided silently along the sidewalk. Chalmers stalked his man, using doorways and shadows as cover, glad of the extra screen the mist provided.

They walked in the direction of the river. The lapping of water against the jetty was an eerie murmuring in the background. Three Fingers dived into a doorway and disappeared.

When Chalmers came up to the doorway, he saw it was the side entrance to a derelict warehouse. The windows were boarded up and a half-obliterated sign swung rustily from broken hinges.

The only sound was the insidious whispering of the black waters about the wharf. The only light, a faint glimmer of yellow from the streetlamp down the block. The world was a chilled greyness—a damp shroud with death lurking everywhere.

Chalmers drew his gun and moved in on the doorway.

CHAPTER 5: SACRIFICE!

Beyond the door, a narrow passageway led into the warehouse. The floor was bare. Footprints in the dust gave him his direction. He followed the prints through an arched portal and found a flight of stone steps leading down to the cellars.

Cautiously he started down the steps. As he descended, the sound of running water became louder, and he guessed he was down to river level, with only the stone wall between him and the swift-flowing Hudson.

The steps ended in another doorway. He stepped through, gun in hand, tensed for action. A heavy curtain hung across the door on the inside. He drew back the curtain and peered into the cellar.

At first, Chalmers had difficulty in making out anything at

all. The room was clouded with the heavy fumes of incense burning in wall brackets. A brazier glowed redly on a dais at the far end. Strange shadows flitted through the room, weaving fantastic patterns. He heard a muttered chant rise from the dim figures standing round the dais.

Chalmers slipped past the curtain and ducked down in a dark corner, his heart thumping wildly. As his eyes became accustomed to the red light filtering through the scented smoke, he was able to identify Dr. Lanson and Three Fingers.

The doctor was standing on the dais, arms upstretched, chanting a monotonous litany. He was garbed in the exotic gown and jewelled turban he had worn the first time Chalmers had seen him. Three Fingers stood behind the doctor, and again his face was obscured by shadows. Chalmers guessed he was preparing to do his ventriloquial act.

Dr. Lanson finished his chanting. A silence fell over the congregation. Chalmers took up a position behind a stone pillar and watched as one man from the crowd went round with a tray. Each person took something from it: some a powder, some a small phial of colourless liquid, some a pipe.

The air thickened. The red glow flickered. Chalmers felt his head spin in that stifling atmosphere. He guessed what it was being handed out. *Dope!*

His eyes roved over the gathering. A dozen in all, not counting the doctor and his assistant, mostly men, but one or two women. Their faces were strained. As they indulged in the narcotic, their faces changed, became more bestial.

Chalmers felt a chill run up his spine. Was the doping the whole entertainment? Or just a preliminary? What was to follow? And where was Ann?

The sound of swift-running water sounded louder through the underground room....

Dr. Lanson raised his arms. In a hollow voice that echoed eerily, he began to speak:

"Tonight the Inner Circle meets for the full ritual. Once more we will indulge in the rites of the Horned One. No longer must

we repress our desires to the dictates of convention."

Chalmers eased back the safety catch on his .45. He had an idea he was going to need it shortly,

The doctor's voice ran on:

"Belchior, messenger of Darkness, are you ready to receive the obeisances of your servants?"

The curious flat voice seemed to come from the thick smoke pouring upwards from the red coals.

"Belchior hears and is ready. Belchior commands a sacrifice!"

"Death—!"

The chorus surged up from eager throats. Drugged faces gleamed in the crimson glow. Chalmers shuddered. If this was what Dudley Brooks had stumbled across in his investigations, it was no wonder that he had been silenced. The flat voice ended its pronouncement:

"—Death unifies all!"

Dr. Lanson moved forward, bright eyes glittering behind the pince-nez. He left the dais and approached an alcove hidden by a black velvet cloth.

He stood in front of the alcove and raised his arms in supplication. His clear-toned voice rang through the crypt.

"In the name of the Horned One, the Shadow, and the Toad that spawns in the outermost Darkness, I dedicate this sacrifice!"

The doctor whipped away the velvet cloth and a terrible chorus surged up from the congregation:

"Belchior's sacrifice!"

Chalmers came to his feet, the blood draining from his face. His lips clamped together in a thin line. His heart pounded wildly...the sacrifice was Ann Stevens!

Lanson brought her from the alcove. She was dressed in a long white robe and her hands were bound; her eyes were wide and mirrored the terror she felt.

Chalmers walked forward mechanically. The assembly was too intent on the girl to notice him. The gun in his hand was

heavy, and a strange light burned in his grey eyes.

Dr. Lanson pulled up a trapdoor in the floor, and the sound of rushing water filled the chamber. They were right over the river. He pushed Ann to the edge, held her there....

Chalmers brought up his gun, trembling with fury.

"You will all participate," commanded the flat voice from the curling smoke.

Lanson stepped back. The drug-takers surrounded Ann, laying hands on her. One push and she would be gone—Chalmers saw it then. Lanson could backmail these people thereafter—they had done the murder, not he!

A smile floated across the doctor's face.

"Now!" he said.

Chalmers acted instinctively. The whole scene was a blur in the red haze before him. Ann—his beloved Ann—was about to die, He fired....

The shot reverberated in the cellar like an avalanche roaring down a mountain slope. Dr. Lanson, a look of utter surprise on his face, reeled back and crumpled in a heap on the floor.

Pandemonium broke loose. Chalmers went on firing automatically, shooting down the dope-crazy fiends who had been about to sacrifice his love.

They shrank back before his burning eyes, leaving Ann alone. He was like a man possessed, with but one purpose in life, to reach the girl. She saw him, and hope dawned in her eyes. She moved back from the trapdoor, straining at the cords binding her.

The Satanists were too shocked by Lanson's death, too full of dope to stop him. Not so Three Fingers. The doctor's assistant, half-hidden by shadows in the background, was instantly in command of the situation. He lunged forward, bringing out a knife.

Chalmers aimed, squeezed the trigger. The hollow click of the hammer warned him the gun was empty. Hurriedly, he began to reload.

Three Fingers seized his opportunity.

"Grab him," he yelled. "Now's our chance—he can't hurt you—get him!'"

He hurled the knife through the air. Chalmers ducked, but not fast enough. The knife grazed his temple, sending him staggering backwards. He dropped the box of shells and they scattered across the floor. Blood streamed down his face, blinding him.

He wiped his face, pushed forward, using the empty gun as a club. White, strained faces surrounded him. Arms pulled him down. He fought them off, forced his way to the girl.

Three Fingers came at him, snarling. They clinched. Ann's eyes were on him, her lips moving in silent prayer.

Chalmers didn't try to avoid Three Fingers. Ignoring the futile grasping of the doped spectators, he sprang at Three Fingers, seized him by the throat.

Slowly, relentlessly, he forced the man's head back. Fists pummelled at his face—he hardly felt them. Suddenly Three Fingers went limp. Sweating, weak from the exertion, Chalmers let him drop to the ground.

There was a confused blur of sound. Sharp voices snapped orders. A volley of gunfire. The sound of feet running across the cellar floor.

Chalmers ignored it all. He grabbed the knife and cut the cords binding Ann. In a moment, she was in his arms, her quivering body taut against him, her lips pressed firmly on his....

A voice said:

"Nice work, son, you've rounded up a gang we've been after for a long time."

Chalmers turned. The speaker was the Captain from the Homicide Bureau, and the place was full of cops. He caught a glimpse of the last of the Satanists being taken away.

His face must have shown surprise for the Captain chuckled.

"If you're wondering how we turned up at just the right moment," he said, "it's because we've had you followed ever since you were turned loose. It was one time the old routine paid off."

Chalmers didn't say anything. He had his arms full.

The Captain looked at Ann.

"You two love-birds oughta get married," he commented drily.

Ann blushed and tried to break free of his embrace.

Burt grinned and pulled her back into his arms.

"That's one swell idea," he said, "let's hunt up a preacher!"

He guessed from the eager pressure of her lips that the idea was all right by her.

THE HOUSE IN THE PINES

The black tarmac shone wetly. A drizzle of rain, so fine as to be almost a mist, coated the empty shelters facing a metallic grey sea and the CLOSED notice hanging from a chain across the entrance to the pier.

Charles Cassidy drove slowly past a dark and silent Fun Arcade, musing: there's nothing so dismal as an end-of-season seaside resort.

It was not surprising there were few people about in the Autumn twilight. Although still early, he switched on his side-lamps. He'd had a couple of drinks with his dinner on the way down, and could do without an accident and a police report. He had enough of a problem already.

Windscreen wipers hissed hypnotically and he needed all his concentration for the road. He cruised by a holiday camp, deserted as any city centre on a Sunday.

The old Ford shuddered a bit; his daily round took a lot out of a car, but now was not the time to buy a new one. He had to straighten himself out first, make a decision. If he quit his job, he had to find another, and preferably one better-paid.

His gaze took in hotels and guest houses lined up like a stage set with nothing behind them. The street lighting had yet to be switched on, and the view had a depressing effect—but he hadn't come here for a good time. What he needed was peace and quiet while he gave serious thought to a future that included neither Imperial Insurance nor that bitch Ogilvie....

When he reached the end of the Promenade, the coast road

appeared even bleaker, with sand dunes reaching to distant chalk cliffs, and a few pine trees scattered among chalets and bungalows. He must be nearly there.

Cassidy had been in his job for almost ten years. Since his wife left him, he'd had no real worries until Miss Ogilvie arrived from Head Office to take over as District Supervisor.

She never left her desk, but expected him to run around working up new business. And she never let up: nag, nag, nag.... Christ, you'd think they were married the way she carried on. He'd reached the point where he couldn't stand her any longer; he was losing sleep and talking to himself in the street.

Cassidy shuddered. He'd seen people like that and avoided them; but now, to become one of them....

So he'd taken a long weekend, Friday till Monday. He was on his own with no pressure of any kind; he had to do some straight thinking, decide what he was going to do.

The Ford's sidelights briefly illuminated a sign on the right— *The Pines*—and he turned in through a gateway. The gates were missing. The drive curved between evergreens to a big house that showed as a gaunt outline against the damp sky, windows shuttered and not a light anywhere. His heart sank.

The voice on the telephone when he made the booking had sounded oddly distorted. Of course, it had been a bad line. At first a man seemed to be insisting that "The Pines" was closed for the winter; then a woman took over, her voice fading in and out.

"It's self-catering—"

"I can look after myself."

"There's nobody else booked for this weekend—"

"I'm looking for a bit of quiet."

"Just make yourself at home—"

"I can manage that."

The price was ridiculously low, and he'd posted a cheque, stopping on the way down to buy easy-to-prepare food at a supermarket: bread, butter and milk, tea and coffee, bacon, eggs, and sausages. And a bottle of vodka.

He didn't intend going far. Perhaps a walk along the beach for fresh air and exercise—if the weather improved.

He parked in front of the porch; the door looked a thick and heavy affair designed to repel invaders. He pressed the bell-push and waited. When no one answered, he remembered he would have the place to himself. He pushed the door and it swung easily on well-oiled hinges. The hall was in darkness and he fumbled for a switch, depressed it, breathed a sigh of relief as a light came on.

He called, "Anyone home?" There was no reply. He carried his suitcase and carton of groceries inside, then drove around the side of the house. These days, he expected vandals every-where.

The garden was unkempt, dripping with moisture. He found a lean-to, screened by bushes, and drove the Ford inside, locked the doors, and put the keys in his pocket.

He walked quickly through the drizzle to the front door and closed it behind him. A passage extended before him; carpeted stairs led to an upper floor. An open door revealed a lounge with a large television set and armchairs.

Cassidy switched on the lights and an electric fire. Cosy. He carried his carton along the passage to the kitchen to put his groceries in the fridge; he opened a cupboard and found a glass.

Back in the lounge he poured himself a drink and turned on the TV. The news was all bad, and the Western that followed didn't interest him. He felt tensed up and took a second drink. It was quiet apart from the gentle susurration of the sea and the wind through the pine trees.

He carried his suitcase upstairs. A passage wandered around the house, which was old and seemed to have had extensions built onto it at different times. There were steps down, and steps up, and sometimes one room led through another; at bends in the passage, mirrors on the wall gave a view around the corner. Cassidy found it confusing, a bit like a maze. Part of the passage might have been outside the house at one time, and roofed over.

He found a bathroom at the back and selected the room next

to it. There was a double bed, a couple of chairs, and wardrobe; his face looked worn and grey in the dusty mirror. He imagined the cleaners didn't bother at the end of season, that he might be the last guest until Spring.

The windows were shuttered and, in the light of a single lamp, the wallpaper appeared faded with a pattern he couldn't quite make out. He changed into pyjamas and poured himself a nightcap, regretting he hadn't thought to buy a paperback in his hurry to get away from her....

He drained his glass and switched off the light. A moonbeam squeezed through a crack in the shuttering to create a strange halo in the mirror.

Cassidy felt restless, and it was a while before he edged into a troubled sleep, only to wake up screaming and sobbing.

"Bitch...what gave her the right to make his life a misery? Why should he have to find another job? She didn't know the work anyway.... She...."

He threw back a tangle of sheets, fumbled for the light switch, and walked up and down the carpet, his teeth grinding. He poured another glass of vodka and drained it at a gulp. Jesus, he'd end up in an alcoholic ward at this rate.

He peered at himself in the mirror. The stubble on his jaw was beaded with sweat—and he saw he was gesturing wildly as he mumbled under his breath.

"Cut it out!"

With an effort of will, he forced himself to stop. Moonlight filtered through a crack in the shutter and the room seemed airless. He opened the door and strolled into the passage, paused.

Was that a voice? He listened. There were no other lights, on but he felt sure he heard a low voice somewhere. Maybe someone else was staying here after all.

As he turned back to his room, he sniffed the air. There was a scent he hadn't noticed before; a light delicate perfume. It became stronger as he inhaled; no longer subtle but blatant, and overpowering in its seductiveness. It pervaded the whole room.

His reflection in the dusty mirror became distorted; it rippled

and shifted to a female face with dark eyes and pouting lips. Cassidy looked behind him. He was alone.

Now he became acutely aware of the wallpaper and recognised the pattern; a series of lips, cupid's bow lips in faded pink. As he stared the pink brightened to a vivid alluring red. And the lips moved.

Christ, he must be closer to a breakdown than he'd thought. His head began to spin and it seemed that the walls puckered and the lips bulged towards him. Inviting scarlet lips.

The lips whispered. His ears strained but the words remained just below his threshold of understanding. Frustrated, he concentrated, imagined....

"Going crazy," he muttered.

The lips on the wall parted wider and mocking laughter crept through the room.

Cassidy flung open the door, crossed the passage to another room and flopped down on the bed. The wall contorted into a pair of lips that loomed over him and he tasted salt.

A whisper tickled his ears. "Why do you hate women, Charles? You must learn better...I'll teach you."

He turned over, face down, and pulled a pillow around his ears. Presently he edged into uneasy sleep.

Cassidy woke late. A mad drummer beat a tattoo inside his skull to an accompaniment of woodwind. Gradually it dawned on him that the noise was a downpour of heavy rain and a gale blowing through the pine trees.

He stumbled into the bathroom and ran hot water into the tub. Jesus, no more late night drinking; that had been some nightmare. His face, reflected in a steamy mirror, showed red marks. Lipstick?

After soaking and dressing, he went downstairs and fried a breakfast of sausage, bacon, and egg. He lingered over a pot of tea as the rain drummed and the wind howled. Well, he didn't have to go anywhere; his time was his own.

He washed up, remade both beds, and made a brief search of the upper floor. He was alone. He wandered down to the lounge,

switched on the fire and the TV. An advertisement for tooth-paste showed a smiling blonde, smooth and shiny as a china-doll...the picture wavered, changed to a dark seductive beauty.

He froze as a stench of perfume came from the set, and then he heard the sultry voice of the night before.

"I like you, Charles, you're amusing. You weren't thinking of leaving me, were you? I can't allow that."

The screen gave a mocking laugh...and the blonde was back, extolling the virtues of Dentashine toothpaste.

In a panic he ran from the lounge to the front door. It was heavy and solid, and though he tugged with all his strength, it refused to open. The door was not bolted. Had someone locked it during the night, not realising he was inside?

He moved quickly around the ground floor, and found there was no other door; unusual in a house of that size. And the windows were either shuttered on the outside, or barred.

Barred? He grew frightened as he imagined what the house might have been used for.

He looked desperately around the hall, and saw a telephone, half-obscured by the wilting leaves of a plant. He picked it up and listened. There was no dialling tone, only a long sigh that could have been the wind. And a familiar voice.

"How nice of you to call me up, Charles! I'm thrilled—"

Cassidy slammed down the receiver, and took the stairs two at a time. There just had to be a way out. It wasn't such a long drop from the upstairs window—he had a vague notion of tying sheets together and fastening one end to a bed.

He went around and around, along passages, through rooms, up and down steps. The place was a maze. And every window was either shuttered or covered by iron bars.

There was no fire escape; that was illegal, wasn't it? He always came back to the staircase above the hall, and the mirror showing a reflection of the empty corridor beyond the bend. Now the glass showed lips puckering from the walls.

He shuddered. The place was a prison, totally enclosed; there was no way out, no escape for him.

He collected his bottle, more than half-empty, and went slowly down the stairs as if to meet his doom. The walls pouted lips ripe for kissing and he shrank away from them. Despair shrivelled his ego.

A soft chuckle floated on the air. A whisper. "I don't give up easily, Charles. You're mine, all mine."

He dropped the bottle and put his hands over his ears and screamed. Presently he recovered enough to pick up the bottle and drain it.

The walls ballooned their ripe red lips. lips that touched his, and he tasted blood. Now he knew what that salty taste had been.

"Charlie, relax. You'll enjoy it...."

He was trembling as the lips pressed harder, and sucked and sucked....

By Spring, when the cleaners came to get the house ready for a new season, all that remained of Charles Cassidy was an empty husk.

THE ORGAN BANK CAPER

"And so, another case came to a satisfying and scientific conclusion...."

John Maracot, scientific detective, perched his lean body on a lab stool, set an egg timer, and toyed with the latest 3-D puzzle. Surely he could do better than seven seconds?

As Maracot finished dictating another memoir, 'Red' Hockney, ace reporter, changed the setting in his machine and said, "Guess I'll call this one *The Invisible Ray Murders.*"

Maracot made a face. "Must you be so crude?"

"That's the sort of title that sells," Hockney defended.

The office receptionist chimed, "Doctor Tobor wishes to consult you."

Maracot brightened immediately, "Send him in."

Doctor Tobor, short and bald, seemed worried as he opened the door and entered the laboratory.

Maracot snitched off the egg timer, and allowed his puzzle to collapse into 2-D. He waved his hand at Hockney.

"This red-headed giant is my biographer, You can speak freely in front of him, doctor."

"I own a private organ bank," Tobor said, and handed Maracot his card.

As Maracot took it, the card lit up with an advertising sign;

Body Re-building by Experts
Used lungs, hearts and limbs
Donors freshly killed to your order

"We're missing some body parts," Tobor said, "despite tight security and armed guards. Some part disappears every night—by now, there's almost enough gone to build a complete person. It's a total mystery."

"Frankenstein lives?" Hockney quipped,

Tobor shuddered. "Don't please! This business has got me believing in spooks."

Maracot frowned and rubbed the side of his aquiline nose. His eyes burned with a zealous fervour.

"Intriguing. Distinctly promising. My recent cases have been mundane—yes, I think I'll take this case."

"The Walking Parts Mystery?" Hockney suggested.

"Must you?" Maracot donned a bullet-proof cape and slouch hat. "Let us proceed to the scene of the crime. Every mystery has a scientific explanation."

They descended to the underground garage where the detective's armoured hovercar waited, already filled with investigative equipment.

"Give directions, doctor," Maracot said as he took the controls.

They arrived at Tobor's organ bank, a solid concrete block with steel bars across smoked glass windows. Tobor pressed his thumb against a scanner and the door opened.

Inside, the air was cool. The two security guards in the hall eyed Maracot warily.

"You needn't stay here tonight," he told them. "My assistant and I will do what's necessary."

They appeared relieved and left quickly, and Doctor Tobor showed him around. Racks of limbs hung from hooks; and hearts, livers, and lungs were displayed in glass jars on shelves.

"A regular butcher's shop," Red Hockney commented.

Tobor pointed at a metal door at the rear. "Our deep freeze."

Maracot checked the doors and windows; all were locked with approved security devices.

"Looks good," he said, rubbing his hands. "All right, doctor, leave it to us. We'll bring my equipment in and set it up. I'll

soon find out what's going on here after dark."

After Tobor had left, Maracot arranged his black boxes at strategic intervals around the organ bank and plugged into the main supply. He switched off the overhead lighting, leaving only a glow of night lights, and brought two chairs from the office.

"Compose yourself, Red. We may have a long wait."

Maracot relaxed in his chair, closed his eyes and practised deep breathing.

Hockney murmured; "Real eerie, this place. Like zombie-land. I'm not too sure you're going to find a scientific explanation for this one."

Maracot's lips curved in a faint smile.

Presently traffic noises faded away. There was only the hum of an air-conditioner. The wall clock ticked into the early hours.

Then came a faint sound.

Maracot's eyes snapped open. He tensed, fully alert as he looked for the source of the sound: The door of the deep freeze opened and a caricature of a man hobbled out.

One leg was longer than the other, the head was set at an angle on the neck and obviously didn't belong to the body. The stomach gaped open.

Maracot heard Hockney's sudden intake of breath and laid a restraining hand on his assistant. He mouthed *Quiet!*

The almost-a-man shuffled slowly along the racks of spare parts, helping himself to this and that, trying bits for size. He fitted something into his stomach.

"Jeez," Hockney muttered. "What's that?"

Maracot suppressed a chuckle. "Alimentary, my dear Hockney!"

Red started to get up.

"Wait!"

The spare part body seemed to have finished equipping itself. It turned and looked about. It saw them, paused a moment, then began to move towards them.

Maracot pressed the switch in his hand and a dazzling blue-white light crackled about the strange figure, completely

encasing it,

"Now you can move, Red," he said briskly. "I've caged it in a network of magnetic radiation. Let's see what we've caught."

He switched on the overhead lighting and walked towards the intruder.

The newly completed body looked back at him with a hunted expression. The mouth opened to make a croaking sound.

"Vocal cords stiff from disuse," Maracot observed. He addressed the intruder. "Well, explain yourself. What are you doing here?"

The words cane slowly. "I am a...visitor...to your world."

"Obviously," Maracot said, unimpressed. "An alien. And, I suspect, an immaterial life form."

"Immaterial...ethereal, yes. To explore your world...I need a body. I built this one."

"Jeez, a do-it-yourself alien," Hockney muttered into his recorder.

"There are others of your kind coming?" Maracot asked.

"Yes—many."

John Maracot smiled with satisfaction.

"I think, my dear Hockney, I shall retire from the scientific detective business. It never did pay, anyway. I shall buy a share in the organ bank and open a tourist agency."

THE CRIME AT
BLACK DYKE

Whistling the latest hit by her favourite female singer, Jo Royal swung her Alfa Romeo around the bend in the road and jammed on the brakes. The narrow country road was blocked by a crowd of women carrying banners and chanting slogans.

She stopped and stared at a demonstration in the heart of rural Shropshire.

A banner read: CHARLIE IS NOT MY DARLING!

The chanting proclaimed: "Stop your pollution, Pearson!"

An angry woman who looked as if she had been crying glared into the car and demanded: "Do you work for Pearson's Pesticides?"

"Not likely," Jo said. "I work for me. Right now I'm heading for—" She glanced down at the map spread across her knees. "—Black Dyke. I'm on holiday and touring, and looking for a hotel to stay the night."

The woman thrust a leaflet through the open window. "Then you ought to know about this."

Jo read the flimsy sheet:

POLLUTION AT BLACK DYKE!

Charles Pearson's chemical factory is dumping poisonous waste in our town canal. Several children are in the cottage hospital, one seriously ill....

"Maybe I did," Jo said, and reached for the Pentax camera on the seat beside her. "I'm a freelance journalist when I'm working."

"That's great—maybe you can get us some publicity. I'm Ann Shephard. I'll guide you into Black Dyke."

She handed her bundle of leaflets to one of the other women, opened the car door, and got in.

"Clear the road, Maureen. I'm taking a journalist to the hospital."

After the women moved aside, Jo drove forward, past the wrought-iron gates of a large country house.

"That's where Pearson lives when he's home," Ann said. "Charles Pearson—you must have heard of him."

"Vaguely," Jo said. "Refresh my memory."

"He reckons he's the Lord of the Manor in this part of the country. His great-grandfather started a small chemical factory. When Charlie took control, he went to the City and came back with money to expand and develop. His factory has done well, selling fertilizers and pesticides all round the world, and he's after a knighthood. He's rich enough to buy people off."

"No one buys me off," Jo said. "Feed me some facts."

The car passed over a hump-backed bridge crossing a narrow canal. The water was scummy, and an unpleasant smell arose from it. Adults patrolled the towpath, chasing children away.

"When I was a kid, we always played along the canal bank," Ann said. "Now, it's too dangerous,"

The road entered a street lined by terraced houses and shops. Black Dyke was a market town, dominated by the tanks and pipes of an immense chemical plant. Jo noted the *Talbot*, a four-star hotel.

The cottage hospital was at the far end of the town, a small modern building. Jo parked in the drive and Ann Shepherd got out, moving at a brisk trot. Jo followed.

A woman was talking to a man in a white coat at reception.

"How is she, Sarah?" Ann asked.

"As well as can be expected," the doctor said quickly.

"What does that mean?"

"She's still seriously ill. I can't allow visitors."

Ann turned to Jo. "This doctor's been bought. Because Pearson paid for this hospital, he thinks it doesn't matter how many of our kids are poisoned."

The doctor looked uneasy. "That's not fair. The town needs this hospital, and without Mr. Pearson—"

"Tough," Jo said. "But life never was simple. Let me see your patient, and maybe I can do something to help."

Jo opened her handbag and selected a card which read:

JO ROYAL
Photo-Journalist

The doctor hesitated briefly, then said: "Very well. We've nothing to hide—you can see her, but that's all. And please leave my name out of this."

"Of course, doctor."

He led the way down a passage and opened a door. It was a small private ward, with a nurse in attendance. A girl of about seven lay in bed, her face pale and her eyes wide open.

"Mummy," she said. "I'm hurting...."

Sarah began to cry, and the doctor gestured them to leave and closed the door.

Ann said angrily, "Are you doing anything for her?"

"Everything we can." The doctor looked unhappy. "Some of those industrial chemicals are very complex compounds."

Outside, Jo said, "Something ought to be done about Charles Pearson."

Ann shrugged. "He's clever. He makes a big thing about avoiding polluting the countryside—and people believe him."

Jo smiled. "Tell me about him. Every man has his weakness...."

* * * * * * *

Jo booked in at the *Talbot* and got Pearson's personal assistant on the phone. It took only a mention of a rumour about a knighthood to Pearson, another mention of a national magazine, and she was granted an interview.

After a breakfast of champagne and pomegranate, Jo drove off to Pearson's country house with camera and a shorthand notebook.

She approached the house slowly, studying the cover. Behind stone walls were a lot of trees and bushes. The windows were high and narrow, with ivy covering the walls. There'd be no trouble getting into the house.

She parked and went up the steps between fluted columns. A uniformed security man with a truncheon at his belt opened the door.

Pearson waited for her in the lounge, beside a drinks cabinet. Jo, wearing a business suit, assumed an appearance of cool professionalism.

Charles Pearson looked like an elderly cherub with snow-white hair, but cold grey eyes revealed another side to his character.

She accepted a sherry and sipped slowly, gazing around the room, aware of a musty smell.

"So, Ms. Royal, what sort of a story are you looking for?"

"A personal story. Your family and background." Jo spoke earnestly. "Your ancestors. How the business started—how you developed it."

Pearson swallowed his sherry in one gulp and stood up.

"Yes, I'm proud of my ancestors, proud of the family home." He indicated the room and its antique furniture with a sweep of his arm. "The Pearsons go back a long way. Right now, my personal assistant is engaged in drawing up a family tree for— you know what. It was my great-grandfather who started it, in a small way of business, of course. That's his portrait over the mantelpiece."

Jo stared at a framed oil painting from which a face peered out through a layer of discoloured varnish. It might have been

a portrait of Scrooge, she thought; a pointed nose, shrivelled cheeks, and thin lips.

"Simon Pearson, painted by Sir Thomas Lawrence. The experts tell me it's worth money. But what's money? I wouldn't part with that painting for a million pounds. When I look at old Simon, I see myself."

Jo had trained herself to estimate measurements accurately, and she jotted down figures in her notebook.

She raised her camera.

"Will you pose for me? Beside the painting."

"With pleasure," he said, proudly,

She took several shots, including one of the painting on its own.

"Our female readers would be thrilled to learn something about your house...."

Pearson gave her a conducted tour, and Jo's camera snapped the detail she needed. The passages were on different levels; doors led off to additions to the original building. There was no alarm system, and no dogs; apparently he relied for security on his thugs armed with truncheons.

He showed her the wine cellar, padlocked. A child could have opened it with a hairpin. At the rear of the cellar she saw a number of old paintings covered in dust.

As she was about to leave, Jo said, "The women of Black Dyke accuse you of poisoning the canal. Some of the town children are in hospital. Would you like to comment?"

Pearson's face coloured with anger. His words cane out like an explosion.

"Absolute rubbish! My factory provides work for the men of Black Dyke. Their hospital was built with my money. Of course I don't pollute their stinking canal. These women are freaks, do-gooders, libbers—stupid! I'll never give in to them. Never!"

Jo Royal smiled.

* * * * * * *

From Black Dykes, she drove back to London and got her film developed. She asked for a large blow-up of old Simon's portrait and took it to a painting friend in Chelsea, who specialized in copying Old Masters.

"Could be Lawrence," Billy Baines said. "Or it might be a copy after him. I'd have to see the original to be sure."

Jo flipped open her notebook and gave him the measurements. "Can you paint me a copy? Exactly as is, brown varnish and all?"

"No problem. I'll do it for you over the weekend. Okay?"

"Okay."

* * * * * *

Jo relaxed aboard her motor cruiser moored on the Thames. On Monday morning she visited Billy Baines again and admired his handiwork.

"It won't pass scrutiny by an expert," he warned.

"If everything goes according to plan, it won't have to," she said. "Now, I want to borrow some tools to remove a canvas and replace it with this."

"I'll want them back."

"Of course, Billy."

Back aboard her cruiser, Jo studied Billy's copy again. Simon Pearson sneered at her from beneath thick brown varnish.

"You're about to become famous, Scrooge," she murmured.

She used the radio-phone to make an overnight booking at the *Talbot*. Then she rang Ann Shephard and invited her to dinner at the hotel.

Her Alfa Romero covered the miles to Shropshire at a comfortable seventy for most of the motorway. She booked in and relaxed in a hot bath, then dressed for dinner.

Over gammon steak, fresh fruit with cream, and coffee, Jo said, "I can do something about Charlie Pearson—but I'm going to need your help."

"Anything," Ann said fervently.

"I'm not going into detail. The less you know the better if the police should ask questions afterwards. What I want is a diversion."

Ann's eyes opened wide as she listened.

"That's easy enough. I'm good at organising demos...."

* * * * * * *

Jo was up early next morning. She dressed in a tracksuit and trainers, checked she had Billy's tools, and the rolled-up canvas in her holdall, and jogged out of town.

At dawn, she scaled the wall surrounding the grounds of Pearson's house. She moved quickly and silently to a tree growing close to the house and shinned up it. She straddled a branch among dense foliage and settled to wait.

Presently she heard chanting, and saw a crowd of women marching along the road. She watched as Ann used a tyre lever to force open the wrought-iron gates. The demonstrators swarmed into the grounds and spread out, carrying banners and chanting a new slogan:

"Poisonous Pearson is a pest!"

A couple of security men ran out of the lodge, and the women scattered among the trees and bushes. A cameraman from a photographic agency was with them, shooting pictures. More security men came from the house, truncheons drawn.

Jo slid down the trunk of her tree and darted into the house. She went directly to the empty lounge, and lifted down old Simon's portrait and carried it to the door. The house was quiet.

She moved along the passage to the steps leading down to the cellar. Her picklock opened the door in seconds and she switched on the light and closed the door after her.

She moved to the rear of the cellar and started work. Taking the old canvas out of its frame, she used pliers to remove the tacks holding the canvas to its stretcher. Then, working quickly, she placed Billy's copy over the stretcher and nailed it in place using steel tacks and a hammer. She used corner wedges to

tighten the canvas, and slid it back into the heavy frame. She used spit to smear dust over the shiny new nails, then hid the portrait among the other paintings stacked at the back of the cellar.

She put Billy's tools into her holdall along with the rolled-up canvas, and took a final look round. There was no sign she had been there. She switched off the light and eased open the door. She heard distant shouting. She relocked the cellar and left the house.

In the grounds she saw a security man hitting a woman with his truncheon. Two other demonstrators pulled him away. The photographer's camera snapped them.

"Get that camera!" another security man shouted.

Jo signalled to Ann, who called, "Everybody leave!"

Ann and Jo ran interference for the cameraman.

"Move," Jo hissed. "Get that photo to the London papers."

She joined the exodus.

* * * * * * *

Aboard her motor cruiser at Chelsea, Jo unrolled the stolen canvas. In places the paint had cracked; a job for Michael Cade, she decided.

She smiled as she looked at the daily papers. The picture of Pearson's security man hitting a woman was on the front page, and Pearson was quoted:

"The guard was overexcited. You must remember that these women were on private property. Of course, my factory has never polluted the canal...the demonstrators stole a valuable painting and I shan't rest until I have recovered it."

Jo typed an open letter to Pearson:

"Your painting will be returned immediately you acknowledge responsibility for the polluted canal at Black Dyke."

She sent copies to all the daily papers and national television studios. It got maximum publicity and a quick answer from Pearson:

"I agree. I am taking steps to avoid further pollution—and will personally see that the canal is cleaned out."

His cherubic face came over well on the screen. He might still get his knighthood, Jo thought. While waiting for Ann to report that the canal was clean again, she took the original to Michael at Cade's auction house.

He inspected the cracks in the surface and said, "There's another painting beneath this, Jo. I doubt if this is a genuine Lawrence, so I'll take a chance and see what's underneath."

Jo heard from Ann and wrote to Pearson, telling him to look in his wine cellar. She had no fear of repercussions; the painting of old Simon was in its original frame and had never left the house. There would be no need to have it examined by an expert.

Later, Michael phoned. "I've got something to show you."

She called at the auction rooms where a painting rested on an easel. Gone was old Scrooge.

She saw an oil sketch of a buxom female nude, painted in glowing pinks.

"A real find," Michael said. "A Rubens sketch for one of his paintings. It'll bring a good price at auction. You know, the real crime at Black Dyke was to cover a Rubens nude with that awful face...."

"Typical," Jo said. "Just like a man."

THE BOOK MISER

Josephine Royal drifted through the crowded apartment, a glass of champagne in her hand, listening to small talk. Chelsea parties tended towards art gossip, and sometimes she picked up a useful piece of information.

There were balloons and streamers, wine and pot, artists, agents, and clients. *Hawkwind* played on the Hi-fi. When it was necessary, she hinted that she represented a media agency.

"Jo!" Her hostess dragged a reluctant young woman towards her. A tweed skirt suggested a visitor from the country. "I want you to talk to Celia—she has a problem. Use the bedroom."

The bed was piled high with coats, but the room was reasonably quiet.

Celia looked embarrassed. "I don't think anyone can help—it's too late. Are you really an enquiry agent?"

"I do make enquiries," Jo said truthfully.

"When she said Jo Royal, I imagined the tough sort of private eye in an American film, and—"

In the wardrobe mirror, Jo's reflection revealed a tall and slender redhead with freckles, wearing a lime-green dress.

"So what's the problem? I don't charge for advice."

"My aunt was robbed. And she's ill and desperately needs money and—"

"Robbed of what? And how?"

"When her husband died, she sold off a lot of old books to raise some money. One of them was a first edition of *A Study in Scarlet* by Conan Doyle, a Sherlock Holmes novel. The buyer

paid fifty pounds, which sounded a lot to her at the time. I've since learnt that it's worth thousands."

Jo shrugged. "Dealers are like that."

"But he's not a dealer! He's a collector, and certainly knew its value." Celia sounded bitter. "He could have afforded to pay the market price."

"There's nothing you can do, legally," Jo said. "A sale is a sale. Let the buyer—in this case, the seller—beware."

"My aunt is dying of cancer and a few thousand would ease the end. I could get her into a hospice. I appealed to this collector—a man named Robert Bradman—and he laughed at me."

"Not nice," Jo said. "If there's something I can do, we'll split the money fifty-fifty after expenses. Okay?"

"Of course. Anything you can get out of that dreadful man will be welcome."

"Where does he live?"

"Number seventeen Willoughby Square."

"I'll take a look at him tomorrow," Jo promised.

* * * * * * *

Willoughby Square was off Park Lane, a garden surrounded by old houses. Number seventeen could have done with a coat of paint. The windows were narrow and curtained. Hiding iron bars? Jo wondered as she went up the steps. The brass door-knocker needed a polish.

She studied the lock while she waited—a modern security lock. When the door opened, on a chain, she held out a card that read:

JO ROYAL
Book Scout

"I'm new to this game," she said, "so you may not have heard of me. But I can give a reference. I hope you'll let me

have your wants list—I do get around, and quite often come across something unusual."

Robert Bradman looked at her tight-fitting jeans and cotton T-shirt and unchained the door.

"Do come in, Ms. Royal."

Jo's gaze swept across the alarm control box in the hall: an expensive model.

As Bradman showed her into his study, she noted the position of the light switch. The room was large and lined with glass-fronted bookcases. She saw rows of old books, each in a clear plastic cover.

Bradman sat at his desk and watched her. He was growing a paunch, his hair thinning and his nose pointed.

Abruptly, he said, "Your reference?"

Jo smiled. "Michael, at Cade's auction house."

He dialed and spoke quickly. The answer satisfied him. "You appear to be genuine—and I like the look of you." He opened a drawer and took out a sheet of paper. "My current list of wanted books."

She ran her eye down the list and commented, "Expensive stuff."

"I can pay—if I have to. Naturally, I prefer to buy my books cheaply if it's possible."

"Naturally. You don't specialize?"

Bradman chuckled. "Only in valuable books. They're a form of investment."

"You don't read them?"

"Hardly! The less handling the better. Straight into a plastic cover, and sealed, is my method."

It was an attitude that Jo despised. Books were meant to be read, not hoarded to sell at a profit. He was a miser, and she was going to enjoy taking money off him.

"It's a point of view," she said, and looked at the bookcases.

A Study in Scarlet, in its original pictorial wrapper, had pride of place in the largest bookcase. She didn't doubt the doors were locked.

"All first editions," Bradman said. "Can I offer you a drink?"

Jo put his wants list in her pocket. "Not now. Another time, perhaps."

"Anytime. I fancy you."

"Sometimes I fancy a man," she said calmly. "And I work occasionally as a topless dancer in a club. Maybe I'll give you a ring."

As she left, she noticed smears of dust. Bradman lived alone.

* * * * * * *

Back aboard the motor cruiser she used as a mobile home, at present moored at Chelsea on the Thames, she used the radio-phone. It took four calls to track down a facsimile that had been produced by the Holmes Society in 1960.

Next day, she collected the copy and sealed it in plastic. A casual glance would reveal no difference.

She visited a locksmith and bought the same model of the lock on the front door of Number 17 Willoughby Square. A burglar friend made her a skeleton key to open any lock of that type.

She enquired about the alarm system at the manufacturers and collected their brochures. She learnt how to stretch it off—and that she had thirty seconds to do so after she opened the door. She had her own set of picklocks for the bookcase.

When she was ready, she phoned Bradman to make a date.

"It's Jo Royal, your friendly book scout. I finish my act at the Brass Nightingale in Soho at eleven. You can pick me up there if you're still interested."

Heavy breathing sounded from the receiver. "I am."

"I like champagne for breakfast," she said, and rang off.

* * * * * * *

Jo arrived early and watched the front door of number seventeen from the other side of the Square. Trees screened her from

view. She did not have long to wait. Bradman came out, locking the door after him.

She waited till he drove away, then went up the steps. She had the skeleton key in her hand and a handbag holding the facsimile dangled from her arm.

She inserted her key and turned it gently, gradually exerting pressure and listening for the tumblers to move. She heard a faint click. She pushed open the door, darted for the control box, and switched off the alarm. Then she closed the front door and took several deep breaths.

She reckoned she had at least fifteen minutes before Bradman found out she wasn't dancing at the *Brass Nightingale*, and returned.

The study door was unlocked, the room in darkness. She switched on the light and put her handbag on the desk. The curtains were already drawn.

She inspected the bookcase, decided it wasn't wired, and got to work with her picklock. The lock was a simple one and opened easily.

She removed the first edition and laid it on the desk, took the facsimile from her handbag and placed it carefully in the exact position. She closed the door and locked it.

She put the valuable original in her handbag, and looked around to make sure she had left no traces of her entry. She switched off the light and shut the study door.

She paused by the control box, glanced at her watch—only seven minutes gone. She opened the front door, inserted her skeleton key, and switched on the alarm.

Outside, she closed the front door and locked it. Only then did she draw a deep breath. The alarm hadn't sounded. She dropped the key in her handbag and went down the steps.

Footfalls sounded and she looked up quickly. A constable, passing on his beat, glanced at her.

Jo smiled. "Goodnight, constable," she said clearly, and walked briskly in the opposite direction.

* * * * * *

Early next morning she delivered the Doyle first edition to Cade's auction house.

"I'm acting for the seller," she said. "There's a reserve price of twenty thousand."

Michael Cade nodded. "No problem. I would expect it to reach a good deal more. Is there some hurry?"

"But, of course."

"We have a book auction next week. I'll add this item to it."

"That'll be fine."

Jo returned to her motor cruiser and used the radio-phone to make a transatlantic call, person to person.

* * * * * *

Cade's main auction room was crowded with dealers and collectors. Jo stood at the back and let her gaze rove over eager faces. Japanese and Americans predominated, and she was pleased to see one face she expected.

She was not so pleased to see Robert Bradman seated near the front. For a moment, she wondered if he suspected. No, it was natural he would want to know what price this copy fetched.

The auctioneer finished with the earlier items. A porter displayed *A Study in Scarlet.*

"Lot thirty-nine. The first Sherlock Holmes novel, published by Ward Lock in 1887. Very good condition, in the original wrapper. "I shall start at twenty thousand."

Someone raised a catalogue.

"Twenty-one thousand pounds I am bid. And twenty-two. Twenty-three. Twenty-four...."

The atmosphere was tense as the price rose. Only Michael Cade, on the rostrum, remained calm.

An American voice joined in: "Twenty-five."

A group of Japanese went into a huddle.

"Twenty-six."

"And twenty-seven."

Jo stopped holding her breath. It was going to be all right. Before long, *A Study in Scarlet* would be in safe hands.

A Japanese said, with obvious asperity, "Twenty-eight!"

The American signaled.

The price rose steadily to a fantastic sum.

Finally Michael Cade looked around the room. "Will no one offer more?" he said, and paused.

The silence stretched. Cade raised his hammer and brought it down sharply. "Sold to Mr. Peretti."

Bradman left his seat and walked towards the exit. He saw Jo, and scowled.

"Rough night?" she asked. One eye was partially closed and he wore a plaster on his face.

"I suppose you think it's funny. The bouncers at the club you sent me to turned rough."

"Obviously you should pick your playmates with more care."

Cade bustled up. "Your check, Jo, less our percentage."

"Thanks."

Suspicion flared in Bradman's eyes. He turned and forced his way through the crowd to the American,

"Let me look at that!" he demanded.

Peretti held tightly to his book.

Jo murmured, "I think he believes it's his copy."

"That so? And me just this minute buying it." Peretti nodded to the big man following him close as a shadow. "Get rid of him, Nick."

Nick moved between them, his hand in his pocket.

Jo said, "You really should be careful who you accuse, Mr, Bradman." Her voice dropped to a whisper. "Mr. Peretti represents the Syndicate—it's their money he's laundering."

THE FOOTPRINTS

The car's heater worked well and George Thornton felt snug and secure in his Volvo estate as he drove along snow-covered country roads. After Mary's long illness and death, he had decided to accept early retirement; he'd been worn down and felt the need for a fresh start away from the now too-large semi he had shared with his wife for a quarter of a century.

A bungalow in the country would suit, he thought, when business took him to the West Midlands that final summer. The unexpected beauty of the Shropshire countryside charmed him; and, as a Sunday painter, he anticipated many hours of pleasure sketching outdoors in fine weather.

It was a relief, too, to get away from mindless office politics. Since moving up here he felt better than he had for many years. And it was doubly pleasant to be away from colleagues who persisted with their irritating jokes about his forgetfulness, likening him to the schoolboy myth of the absent-minded professor.

Of course, he'd always been a dreamer; but, he informed himself smugly, an organised dreamer. He never forgot the important things in life. He felt pleased he'd obtained all the items on his shopping list, and was confident of surviving the winter even if his recently acquired bungalow should become snowbound.

He admitted he should have left Birmingham earlier, but was not worried. Traffic was light, the tyres gripped well, and he was in no hurry. He was glad he'd decided against taking

the motorway. The deserted countryside lay under a blanket of blue-white snow—he switched off the wipers now it was no longer falling—and the evening sky was clear with a purplish-grey tinge. A full moon lit up bare hedgerows.

He was not pleased when the car's powerful engine gave a discreet cough and died and he coasted to a halt. A single glance at the gauge told him he had run out of petrol, and he scolded himself for forgetting to fill the tank in Birmingham before setting out for home; he reminded himself to add 'petrol' to his next shopping list.

Now he wished he had stuck to the motorway. These small country roads were deserted after dark, and he could not remember passing a garage. He was a long way from home and stranded in country he did not know well.

George Thornton sighed, switching off the headlamps but left side and rear lights burning. He opened the door and got out; the evening air was still and not remarkably cold. He buttoned his short car-coat, took a plastic can from the back, and began to walk. Somewhere there had to be a garage, a house, a passing motorist who would help. He stepped out briskly, not once looking back.

The road was just wide enough for two cars, set down in a rural landscape, the fields snow-covered and unmarked, the branches of trees bare. He swung along, light-hearted, humming a carol. The snow was crisp and crunchy underfoot, and he walked for half-an-hour before he saw ahead the shadow-black shapes of buildings. and quickened his pace.

As he came to the village, dark and silent, composed only of a scattering of cottages and a public house, he saw that doors had been replaced by rusting sheets of corrugated iron and windows boarded over and his heart sank. It was a sign of the times; with industry in the Midlands failing, the inhabitants had gone. The village proved to be derelict, and he walked through it and out the other end, continuing through the lonely countryside.

The night was still and silent with no breath of wind stirring; he saw no sign of nocturnal animals, nor did he hear the cry

of a bird. This was an empty land, bleak and lifeless. The only sounds he was aware of he made himself as he crunched through a crust of snow; the steady pulse of his heart, the regular susurration of his breathing, the swish of coat against trousers. And those sounds seemed strangely muffled as though his ears were stuffed with cotton wool.

The view reminded him of a painting he had once planned; to be called "Winter Evening," the picture would have this same windless air, the same gaunt branches projecting to a cloudless sky, the same sweep of snowy fields rising to distant hills.

There was not even a farmhouse to be seen. He might have been the only man left alive, cut off from all contact with his own kind. He could imagine himself inhabiting the empty landscape he'd planned, a solitary figure, almost an afterthought.

He trudged on till he came to a fork with a signpost. The name burned into dark and weathered wood that pointed along the road was: *Sutton St. Mary*. He's never heard of the place. The left-hand arm of the post bore the legend: *St. Mary's House*, and indicated a narrow footpath.

He was about to proceed along the road when he caught sight of a glimmer of light in the distance, far away down the left fork. A house, he thought, with the chance of getting some petrol.

He took the footpath. Here the snow was deeper and came over the tops of his shoes. He began to hurry, keen to see a human face once more. He climbed over a stile, the plastic can banging against his leg. Presently a grey stone wall loomed ahead, topped with an icing of snow, and he followed it to a pair of wrought iron gates that stood ajar. The light was clearer now and a drive curved through parkland towards a large house. He walked beneath the shadow of leafless trees and the park seemed desolate, the snowscape smooth and unbroken.

The house, as he approached, appeared impressive, with stone steps leading up between columns to an ornate porch and door. A dignified house with wings on either side, tall windows, and even taller chimneys. It looked new by moonlight but, of course, it couldn't be; possibly it was a renovated manor house.

He wondered who could afford such a showpiece.

Immediately before the house was a terrace; on one side of the drive, a snow-covered lawn swept down to a yew hedge; on the other side, beyond a sunken garden with a sundial, the lawn reached to the dark and unruffled surface of a small lake.

Light blazed from the windows, casting a soft radiance over the land. The silence was oppressive, the apparent lack of life frustrating. Even if the owners were absent, surely a house this size must employ servants?

George Thornton stepped onto the terrace and looked in at one of the tall windows. The interior was obviously a ballroom, for he saw a polished wood floor and ornate blue-and-gold chairs lined up along the walls. Chandeliers sparkled with light and, beyond open double-doors, he caught a glimpse of a great staircase.

The sight brought back a memory; Mary had been a keen ballroom dancer. He was struck by a further coincidence: Sutton had been her maiden name.

He turned away, hearing only the sound of his own breathing, the normal beating of his heart. Then he noticed a line of footprints approaching; prints made by a pair of woman's shoes. He saw them distinctly, one imprint forming before his eyes, then another, coming towards him up the drive.

He stood still, holding his breath and his eyes bulging, for he could not see the person making the prints. His muscles tensed and his scalp prickled as he watched the footprints in the snow, watched them silently pass him by, only a few yards away. He imagined he smelt a familiar perfume. The footprints mounted the steps to the porch and still he saw no one.

He felt cold as stone and his legs shuddered as if the strength were being drained from them. After a moment, the door opened on soft light and warmth and then closed again, shutting him out.

George Thornton felt unnerved and his heart pistoned against its cage of ribs. He stared hard at the snow and the unwavering line of footprints. And he looked behind him and choked, and

shock turned to fear. Hesitantly he moved a few paces towards the porch, watching the ground closely, and began to whimper.

His shoes left no impression; the carpet of snow remained unmarked where he walked. And he was filled with the suspicion that there must be something else he had forgotten, something important.

DOWNMARKET

Metal links rattled as Jimmy tugged uselessly at the heavy chain shackling him to a railing in the market place. The padlock was big and heavy. Lifting his head, he saw that the hands of the church clock stood at ten after three, so he'd been here for two hours.

Some joke.

A round moon gilded the deserted square silver between shifting shadows. The breeze that disturbed Autumn leaves and rustled a plastic bag chilled his thin teenaged body. At least it wasn't raining—and a good job Winter hadn't arrived.

He'd seen no sign of life, apart from a ginger cat, since they'd chained him to the railing. The cat paused to sniff at his boots, then moved on. In Summer, there might have been a pair of lovers to release him. The beat copper hadn't been testing doors either, and that was strange.

Jimmy looked past the shuttered stalls to the dark windows of shops and offices bordering the market. He still had hours to wait before the early workers arrived for breakfast at the café. And he was afraid.

He felt betrayed, and desperate, with only one aim: to survive the night. And he'd thought Mary liked him.

The Market House, where Clay the supervisor, had his office, was a pale shape in the centre of the square. Jimmy raised his gaze to the plinth in a niche beneath the eaves, where a stone figure brooded over the market.

He'd never taken much notice before; who looks closely at

some old statue? It was grey and tarnished. Now he saw that the figure was grotesque, tall as a man, with wings folded about a skeletal figure and hog-like snout. A single blank eye seemed to stare directly at him, and he shivered.

He gave a start: had it moved? That had to be his imagination.

* * * * * * *

Napoleon Jimson was a natural coward. When threatened, he relied on his long spindly legs to get him out of trouble.

He'd always been able to outrun the bullies at the Home, to dodge and swerve around his tormentors. His name had caused a lot of aggro; he hated it, and never forgave his mother for inflicting it on him. Not that he remembered her; soon after his father had unloaded her, she'd unloaded him.

Kids can be cruel, and it wasn't only boys who laughed as they chanted:

"Nap, Nap,
What a sap.
Takes the rap,
Gets the strap!"

He wanted only a quiet life, to be left alone, but this time he hadn't run fast enough.

* * * * * * *

The hands of the church clock moved slowly towards the quarter hour. It was going to be a long night. The wind had freshened, moaning through the branches of trees, bringing him the ripe smell of spoilt fruit.

Jimmy looked beyond the stalls to a row of old buildings sandwiched between the new; an ancient arcade cut between the pub and a pizza parlour. There came a small movement; only a

rat at the rubbish.

He tugged ineffectually at the chain. Clay hadn't made any mistake; the handcuffs dug into his skinny wrists and tightened as he struggled. The chain was solid and double-wrapped about the railing. He could move, but not far.

The clock chimed. He sensed the weight of the statue's gaze, heavy as granite, and looked up. The shadowed figure had unfurled its wings. He blinked, and a cloud passed across the face of the moon, blotting out the impossible.

He waited, shivering in the darkness, imagining the sound of beating wings.

When the cloud passed he saw that the niche was empty, the strange figure gliding in a circle on outstretched wings. He cried out in shock and it changed course, swooping towards him and growing larger.

* * * * * *

When he ran away from the Home, he hitched a lift to London and moved into one of the cardboard cities. He called himself 'Jimmy' if anyone challenged him. It was winter and the home-less huddled together.

He was never work-shy, but all he could get was a part-time job minding a street barrow when the owner adjourned to the pub. He lived on pasties and chocolate bars; he'd always had a craving for chocolate.

The unemployed didn't bother him. It was the others: the winos and perverts, the addicts and pushers. And the muggers.

Three of them found him late one evening in a shopping mall. "You gotta chance to share a few quid with your old mates, Jim."

As they closed in, light flashed off a blade and he was off and running; he had strong legs and long strides. In the Spring, he left London for the south.

* * * * * *

The figure glided in to land no more than a few yards away, apparently as light as a feather. It had to be hollow. It furled its wings and stood motionless, watching him. Jimmy began to shake.

The thing, whatever it was, looked formidable, scaly, and the gaze of its single eye skewered him like a lance. Its smell reminded him of a cesspit he'd once almost stumbled into, and he stared in disbelief at the overlapping plates thick with bird droppings.

Then it moved towards him on short stubby legs, talons clicking on the cobblestones. It approached boldly, snout lifted, sniffing the air.

Disbelief gave way to terror as he failed to convince himself it was only someone wearing a mask. In a frenzy of fear he wrenched at the chain holding him prisoner. The cuffs tore his wrists and he ignored the pain and blood as he tried desperately to run away.

The figure waddled nearer, bringing its stench close, open snout within inches of his face.

Jimmy sobbed.

* * * * * * *

He didn't need to go far, only to a small town somewhere between London and the coast where a willing worker was appreciated. They called him a porter and worked him hard, fetching and carrying boxes and crates all day and clearing up afterwards.

The market stalls had gaudy awnings of red and white stripes and they were busy. He had little time to pause between errands. It was "Jim, more cauli here" and "Fetch another crate of bananas quick."

By nightfall he was exhausted but happy. The job didn't pay much, but the stallholders saw he didn't go hungry.

He came to like the smell of fresh fish and oranges, the sight of colourful fabrics snapping in the breeze. He enjoyed the

cheerful market cries. 'Sixty a pound mushrooms. Fresh today, best beetroot!'

The recession hadn't affected this market; the traders had a satisfied air of prosperity, raking in cash as fast as Jimmy could wheel up another barrowload of produce. And he made friends. At least, he thought of them as friends....

* * * * * * *

He backed away as far as the chain allowed and the stinking grey figure followed him. The smell was so strong it threatened to choke him, and he tried to hold his breath.

He tugged at his chain and dreamt for a moment that the whole railing moved.

Talons reached out to grasp him, the way a miser reaches for gold. Jimmy wished he'd never run away from the Home, never left London. He wished he'd accepted the chocolates Mary had offered, now scattered over the ground and out of reach. He wished for...anything but this.

He expelled his breath in a rush. "Get away—leave me alone!"

* * * * * * *

Clay, the market supervisor, was about thirty with a craggy face and surprised Jimmy with his subtle sense of humour. He gave the nod when Mary asked if he could be kept on as their regular porter.

Big Ernie, who ran the fish stall, treated him all right in spite of his size; he seemed a gentle giant.

Mary was older, perhaps forty. She ran a second-hand book-stall and took to Jimmy as if he were a long-lost son. She clucked over him and gave him comics to read.

"There's a shed, just off the square, where we keep barrows and stuff," she told him. "You could sleep there in the summer."

So he moved in, made himself a nest of old sacks, and every-

thing was fine till the night they came for him.

* * * * * * *

It ignored his words. Talons drew him into a close embrace. He shuddered at their touch and, desperate, thrust at the figure with his hands in an attempt to push it away.

The scales felt cold and hard as stone, slimy with bird droppings. He couldn't budge it, and shuddered. The talons tightened as if intent on crushing his thin body. Jimmy screamed his despair.

* * * * * * *

During his last day, he'd noticed sly looks in his direction; traders exchanging a nudge and a wink. And overheard whispers that made him uneasy.

"After all, it's only once a year."

When the stalls closed and the clearing up began, Clay, Mary, and Big Ernie surrounded him.

"Forget that today, Jimmy," Clay said. "Someone else can do it—we're taking you for a slap-up meal."

"You deserve it," Mary said quickly. "It's a sort of celebration."

"Yeah, an anniversary. For the market."

They took him to the pizza parlour. "Anything you like, Jimmy," Ernie said. "Anything at all. No limit."

He had three toppings on his pizza, chocolate gateau to follow, and a large Coke. It was the best meal he'd ever had and when, later, he crawled into his bed in the shed, he quickly fell asleep with a smile on his face.

* * * * * * *

Stiff wings enfolded him, holding him close, and talons dug into his flesh. Jimmy thought wildly of comic book heroes,

but there was not one around to save him. The market square remained silent and empty; he was alone with his nightmare.

A scream was strangled in his throat. He tried to wipe his hands clean, made them into fists to beat on the scaly hide. He might as well have pummelled a cliff face.

The hog-like snout descended and, gently, grey lips touched his.

* * * * * * *

Perhaps it was the slight sound as the shed door opened that woke him. Or moonlight falling across his face. He was instantly alert, scrambling out of his nest and ready to run; he always slept in jeans and tee-shirt.

"Take it easy, Jimmy," a familiar voice said. Clay's face showed pale in the cold light.

"What's wrong?" His pulse was beating faster.

"Nothing's wrong," Mary said, appearing behind the supervisor. "We want you to come outside, that's all."

Jimmy hesitated. He needed to trust his friends, but he had a bad feeling about this visit. He started to run, swerving around them to reach the door, and Big Ernie's arms wrapped about him and he knew it was hopeless. Ernie had the strength of a bear.

"I haven't done anything wrong," he protested.

"Of course you haven't," Mary said quickly. "You're a good boy."

Ernie lifted him and carried him with ease, outside to the square, to one of the railings. Clay snapped on handcuffs and chained him to a railing.

"Why?" He was nearly in tears. "Why are you doing this?"

Mary looked sadly at him. "You'll be helping all of us. All the traders. All your friends."

She offered an open box of chocolates. "These will help."

He looked at her with suspicion. "What are they? Drugs?"

"Just something to help you."

"I don't do drugs." He knocked the box out of her hand, scattering loose chocolates over the cobblestones.

Clay let out a sigh. "That's it then. Come away, Mary."

The three of them left him chained to the railing, crossed the square and disappeared into the arcade. Their footfalls echoes and faded. Then he was alone in the silent market, waiting.

* * * * * *

The lips felt rubbery and he gagged on a vile stench. His arms imprisoned, he was forced backwards over the iron railing till it seemed his spine would snap. He looked up into a single unblinking eye.

The thing sucked, like mouth-to-mouth resuscitation in reverse, slowly at first and then harder until Jimmy's tongue was pulled from its root, choking him. Pain disabled him and he was close to fainting,

As if tempted by a delicacy, the snout sucked greedily with the power of an industrial vacuum cleaner.

This can't be happening, Jimmy thought frantically, but the pain was real. His lungs tore loose and came up through his mouth, his last breath a ragged gasp, and still the suction increased.

"Like I once sucked out a bird's egg," the thought came before he blacked out.

Then his heart was in his mouth, his brain wrenched from its bony cage. Bones splintered and the marrow sucked out. When he was drained, the thing spread its wings ready for flight; gorged and heavy, it wobbled on stumpy legs in the moonlight before it took off.

* * * * * *

Pre-dawn, before anyone else was about, Clay removed the padlock and chain. Mary collected the discarded clothes, and Big Ernie pushed the empty skin into a plastic bag and tossed it

into a waste bin.

They gazed up at the satisfied figure in its niche above the Market House, sure now that they could look forward to another good year.

KNIFE FOR A CANARY

It was only the third time he had used the knife. The first two occasions had been strictly business—this time it was a pleasure.

Johnny Quinn thrust the tip of his tongue between nicotined teeth. His slight figure nestled in a raincoat and his eyes, set in a pale thin face under a derby hat, glittered viciously. Damp fog eddied and swirled around him, blotting out the lamps of Soho.

He crouched to wipe the blade on her dress. "Two-timing bitch," he slurred, tongue still between his teeth.

She was petite, with an hour-glass figure in a crimson gown. As she sprawled on the pavement at his feet, blonde hair tangled and awry, Stella looked an innocent—no longer the sex-kitten of the *Club Roma*.

"The canary will sing no more," Johnny Quinn murmured.

He pushed a cigarette between his lips and listened to the tinny, far-off traffic noises filtering through the fog. Suddenly, he straightened, ears alert. He grew wary, sensing the presence of someone close by.

The toe-caps of his sharply-pointed Italian shoes nudged her briefly as a whisper of sound rolled out of the fog: "Johnny... Johnny Quinn."

He jerked the cigarette from his lips, tearing sensitive skin, and crushed it. There was no mistaking the menace in that voice, nor the voice itself. Fat Reuben. Johnny took two nervous steps to his left, avoiding the spreading pool of blood, and pressed his back against the wall, knife extended horizontally before him. It

was a heavy blade, and broad, curving to a point.

He checked his breathing, peered into the fog. Fear gnawed like a rat at his spine. This was worse than the cops...he'd once seen Fat Reuben at work.

"I'm coming for you, Johnny."

Johnny Quinn shivered, imagining that gross figure, bloated, enormous, working a bicycle chain through fingers encased in chamois leather gloves. Reuben was an artist with the chain. It did Johnny no good at all to recall the face of a victim, ribbons of flesh hanging like macaroni.

He moved off, a silent shadow. The grey-white shroud hanging over the street was a clammy thing, clammy as fear itself. He lunged with his blade, meeting no resistance, and a fat chuckle echoed eerily.

"Nervous, Johnny?"

Hell, he must be close! Johnny Quinn whirled round, striving to suppress the rasping sound of his own breathing. His heart hammered like an overworked engine. And he could not see a damn thing.

All this, he thought bitterly, because of Stella....

Stella Marguerite she had called herself when first she appeared at the club. Johnny remembered the night clearly. He had taken one look at the figure under a brief, tight-fitting gown, and wanted her—and she had smiled back as she circled the close-packed tables, vocalizing a hot number.

The canary was new, the regulars dazzled, and Johnny got in fast. When she finished her act, he called, "That was the real thing, baby. How about joining me for a drink?"

He remembered, her eyes had been just a shade calculating as she answered: "Don't mind if I do, mister."

As they drank together, he slid a hand over bare shoulders.

She brushed it casually away. Very casually. He hadn't stayed brushed off for long, and word soon passed around that Stella was Johnny's girl.

Life became very pleasant for Johnny...until the night Fat Reuben lumbered across the room and splayed soft white hands

over their table. He stared into the vee of her gown and licked pudgy lips. He didn't bother looking at Johnny.

He said, "Three's a crowd," and pulled up a chair.

Johnny's protest was half-hearted. He was small-time, and knew it. Reuben was Mr. Big. He moistened his lips, mumbled "Stella's my girl."

Through cigar smoke and muted chatter, the beat of a Mersey combo, he glanced at her. And Stella, cool as ice, parroted, "He's right, Johnny, three's a crowd. Why don't you take a walk?"

There was nothing he could do about it, not then...but as he stumbled away, his knuckles whitened round the haft of his knife.

Reuben was huge, a good six feet and nearly as wide. Gland trouble made him that way, and the sheer weight put an enormous load on his heart. It was common talk at the Roma that he took pills for the least exertion. He was going to need a lot of pills to cope with Stella....

Johnny wished he'd drop dead right now.

He soft-shoed away from the door porch, smelling the spicy tang of Cypriot cooking, and hit a dustbin. The galvanized-iron lid clattered to the pavement, reverberating. He froze.

"You shouldn't have knifed her, Johnny," purred the voice of Fat Reuben. "You shouldn't have done that."

The voice was without direction. It could have come from anywhere. Johnny Quinn hesitated, terrified by thoughts of Reuben's chain. His saliva, when he swallowed, tasted sour.

The fog thinned a little. Now he saw a gargantuan bulk emerge from swirling white wreaths. He ran, sobbing, into the next dense patch.

A quiet laugh followed him. "Think I can't see you, Johnny? That knife of yours is a dead giveaway—flashes like a beacon!"

Johnny Quinn hurled the heavy blade from him, and immediately regretted his impulse. He heard it ring metallically as it hit the road, heard a fat chuckle behind him.

There was no jealousy in him now, only fear that gripped like a vice. He ran blindly, in a panic, unable to face Reuben's chain.

He halted abruptly. The fog was thicker and he was uncertain of his bearings. He reached out a hand, fumbled at old brick-work. He knew he'd made a bad mistake...he was in a blind alley, short and narrow, with high walls and no exit.

He turned on flat heels, desperate, waiting.

"This is it," Fat Reuben whispered. "The end of everything."

Johnny Quinn slid his back along the wall, shrinking from that whip-like voice. He came to a dead end, stopped. There was nowhere to go.

And out of the curling grey mist shuffled a monstrous figure. He saw a moon face, yellow chamois gloves, and an arm upraised to strike. He heard the frightening downward swish of the chain and covered his face with his hands. Pain lanced up his arms, and he flung them away. Again the steel chain lashed down and he screamed, tasting blood and grease...then a great weight fell against him, bearing him to the ground.

Half-buried, pinned by twenty stone of fat, he listened to the wheezing gasp of Reuben's breathing.

A tortured voice came: "The pills, Johnny...my heart...in my pocket...."

Johnny wriggled free, dipped a hand into Fat Reuben's coat pocket. He found a flat, round box, pulled it out—and hurled it far into the fog.

"The end of you," he said, and laughed.

He kicked Reuben on the face and stepped past. Maybe this was his lucky night after all, if he could find the knife again and press Fat Reuben's prints to it.

Carefully, he retraced his steps. His hands dripped blood and he wound his handkerchief round them, ignoring the pain. The knife first; later, he would see a doctor.

He was almost to the end of the alley when car noises pierced the fog, a slamming of doors and pounding of feet. A whistle blasted close by.

Johnny Quinn ducked into a doorway as orange headlamps swung by, shivered at a passing voice. The voice of the law.

"...the bastard can't be far off. Spread out and keep looking.

She was on special duty at the *Roma*, trying for evidence to convict Reuben. The first time ever a police-woman's been killed...."

"There'll be no let-up on this one!"

CARDILLO'S SHADOW

Mr. Cardillo was afraid of his own shadow. He did not, of course, tell anyone of his fear; that would have been tantamount to admitting mental instability, and Mr. Cardillo shuddered at the thought of confinement in a psychiatric ward. Nevertheless, his fear remained.

So nervous a man as Mr. Cardillo should not have lived alone in the old brownstone house on Cypress Hills. For one thing, the house had a bad reputation and was avoided by the local inhabitants; for another, it was too close to the cemetery to assuage his morbid fears. In appearance, Mr. Cardillo was thin and pale with a high forehead and watery blue eyes, and he habitually wore tight-fitting clothes of faded black that exuded a faint musty odour.

He did not feel lonely, for he was a man given to solitude; he enjoyed the silent hours spent with his books in the dusty library—enjoyed, too, the feeling of companionship his shadow gave him. At high noon, it was an intense black blob very close to his heels, like a faithful hound; at evening, it stretched to a thin, flat counterpart of himself, faintly grey in the dim light.

Mr. Cardillo was on good terms with his shadow; it sat when he sat, walked when he walked, slept when he slept. Sometimes, Mr. Cardillo would bunch his fists and wiggle his fingers so that his shadow took on the form of some animal on the wall of his library; then he would talk to it, as solitary people will, first conjuring up a dream-image. Only, Mr. Cardillo used his shadow. Like Mary's lamb, everywhere that Mr. Cardillo went

his shadow was sure to go—until one day....

Mr. Cardillo was never quite certain when it was he first noticed the discrepancies in his shadow's behaviour. For several days now he had been conscious of some slight irritation, without being able to place his finger on its exact cause. It seemed is if, from the corner of his eye, he caught his shadow indulging in a play of its own; yet when he looked, there was nothing unusual.

He dismissed the idea as fantasy, shrugging his thin shoulders—and vas unduly relieved when his shadow shrugged in sympathy. Later, walking up the hill from the village, he noticed his shadow was blacker than normal for the time of day. It was almost as if it had gained in strength.

He stood quite still in the waning sunlight, staring down at the ground and the flat, black form reaching out to his feet. Instantly his shadow was still. Mr. Cardillo raised his free hand and wiggled his fingers; the shadow copied his movements, but without its usual instantaneous obedience. There was a time lag, as if it were reluctant to perform his bidding.

Uneasy in his mind, Mr. Cardillo dropped his arm and cried out in astonishment, for the arm of the shadow continued upward till the hand reached its face; there, the shadow placed a thumb to its nose and extended all four fingers in a gesture of ridicule and contempt.

Mr. Cardillo closed his eyes, opened them again to find the shadow copying his posture with meticulous care. He blinked; had he imagined that fantastic happening? He plodded onward up the hill, carefully watching his shadow for further signs of insubordination, but he reached the brownstone house without any recurrence of the abnormal.

That evening Mr. Cardillo became obsessed with the idea that his shadow played tricks on him when his back was turned. He paced the library carpet, apparently absorbed in thought; then he would whirl about in an attempt to catch his shadow in the act of some disrespectful gesture. He never succeeded, but the idea that his shadow enjoyed a life of its own persisted in his mind.

"Damnit," said Mr. Cardillo aloud to himself, "it's my shadow—it must do what I do!"

The idea that his shadow might not always faithfully reproduce his own actions irritated Mr. Cardillo; he felt like a man whose wife is unfaithful. But he was not yet afraid—the fear did not begin until the next day....

Mr. Cardillo was in the habit of using a shortcut through the cemetery. The setting sun dropped a bloody shroud across bone-white tombstones, and the dark foliage of cypress trees shivered in a cool evening breeze, patterning the unweeded path with shifting shadows. An owl hooted its melancholy call from high up in the church tower.

Pursuing his course towards the brownstone house and the seclusion of its library, his conscious thoughts absorbed by the abstruse research paper he was engaged upon, Mr. Cardillo was alarmed to notice a slight but persistent tugging at his ankles. He glanced down, thinking to free himself of an entangling brier, and found nothing; he was standing in short grass and his legs were quite free of any encumbrance.

He frowned and walked on. The tugging at his ankles grew stronger as he approached a newly dug and yet-empty grave, the upturned clay wet and heavy and glistening. It was then he became aware that his shadow reached from his feet to the empty grave. With mounting horror, he conceived the idea that his shadow was trying to pull him into the pit.

He stood quite still, pale of face and heart beating faster, deliberately resisting the insistent tugging at his ankles. His shadow, long and flat and darker than it should be with some newfound strength, stretched out to merge with the intense blackness dropping away into the empty grave. It seemed, to Mr. Cardillo, there was something peculiarly obscene in the way his shadow strained against the fetters of his ankles, eagerly seeking to join its fellows in the world of darkness.

Terrified, Mr. Cardillo hurried past the open grave, dragging his reluctant shadow after him. His high forehead was dam with a cold sweat and his limbs trembled; he reached the front door

of his house and fumbled in his pocket for the key. So badly did his hand shake that it was fully five minutes before he got the door open—and, all the while, there was a frightful tugging at his ankles, urging him back to the newly-dug grave in the cemetery.

Mr. Cardillo slammed the door behind him, and bolted and leaned against it, quivering with the weakness of a newborn kitten. When he reached the library, gone was all thought of a pleasant evening's research; he lit the lamp and surreptitiously studied his shadow.

He casually strolled the width of the room, watching the thin dark shape on the carpet; he sat down, crossed his legs; he raised his arm, lowered it. His shadow repeated the performance, this time without obvious reluctance. In fact, it seemed as if the shadow knew his thoughts, so quickly did it respond. It might almost have been burlesquing him, caricaturing his motions with devilish glee. Mr. Cardillo shuddered; there was now no doubt in his mind that his shadow had, in some uncanny way, become imbued with life—and that it was beginning to exert an influence over him.

Sleep was impossible. Mr. Cardillo lay on his bed, quaking with fear at the thought of the black shape beside him, a monstrous Siamese twin. He shuddered his way through the night hours to a tormented dawn.

It occurred to Mr. Cardillo that, perhaps, his was not the only shadow to rebel against its subordinate role in the scheme of things. For one terrible moment he had a vision of a world in which living shadows fought an unceasing battle with the material beings who gave them existence, a battle in which the shadows gained supremacy over the human race. Mr. Cardillo left the seclusion of his brownstone house for the bright sunlight of sanity with more than usual haste.

He spent the morning walking the streets of the village at the foot of the hill, maintaining a careful watch on the shadows of passers-by. Dark shapes danced on the cobblestones, simulating the actions of their human counterparts and, though he studied

closely the fantasy of shadow-play. Mr. Cardillo was forced to acknowledge he could discern no discrepancies in the behaviour of these other shadows.

It was then, in the warm sunlight, that Mr. Cardillo began to have doubts of his mental balance. He must, he told himself, have imagined it all. He flinched, rejecting the obvious course of visiting a psychiatrist, and plodded back up the hill to the lonely brownstone house.

Mr. Cardillo paused, from time to time, to put his shadow through its paces—and on every occasion, it obeyed instantly and correctly. There was no hesitation, no hint of rebellion, so deferential to his slightest whim did the shadow appear, that Mr. Cardillo wondered if he had imagined its previous mockery of his actions.

He reached the gate leading through the cemetery, stood hesitating. He felt loath to pass that empty grave, even in daylight, as he remembered the dreadful tugging at his ankles. but be was tired, and the shortcut saved a further twenty minutes' walk. Surely he need fear nothing in the bright afternoon sunlight? Mr. Cardillo opened the gate and entered the cemetery.

Once be had closed the gate behind him, the sun seemed to lose its reassuring warmth; a chill wind whispered through the cypress trees as he hurried along the path. Tombstones took on the ghastly aspect of yellowed molar stumps set in grim jaws, waiting to devour him.

Mr. Cardillo's feet moved with urgent speed, and his shadow danced before him, black and strong and eager. The newly dug grave with its pyramid of heavy clay loomed ahead; the shadow reached out dark arms, avidly seeking the cradle of its evil life.

Mr. Cardillo checked in mid-stride, ice-cold and stiffening with fear. Before his horrified eyes, the shadow writhed and stretched in a way that bore no resemblance to his own still and petrified form. The dark shape lengthened till its hands reached the edge of the grave; groping fingers crawled over the crumbling brink, secured a tenacious hold in the heavy clay soil.

There came a sudden, vicious jerking at Mr. Cardillo's

ankles, and he felt himself being drawn steadily nearer the open pit. He dug in his heels, resisting his shadow's attempt o pull him towards the grave; he strained against the dark thing on the round, shuddering at its hideous life. The branch of a tree brushed his face, and he grabbed it, his thin hands clutching the branch so tightly he bruised the skin over his knuckles. He held on grimly, fighting his shadow more desperately than any than ever fought a human enemy. Whether he could have won that terrible tug-of-war, Mr. Cardillo could not even guess; his shadow was far from exhausted when it released its hold on the edge of the rave. It snapped back at him, like puppet on elastic, writhing in the old bright sunlight, clawed hands reaching for his throat.

Stumbling in mad flight, Mr. Cardillo raced for his house, ran before his shadow as thin dark hands sought to choke the life from him. He crashed through brier and tangle of weeds, sobbing in terror, white-faced and trembling; he escaped the grinning tombstones and collapsed against the front door of his house.

The sun began to warm him again and, when he looked, his shadow was close at his heels, copying his gestures with open mockery, as if it knew its power was increasing and need no longer bother with the pretence of lifeless subordination. Mr. Cardillo went into his house and locked himself in.

Sunlight flooded through the library windows, and Mr. Cardillo's shadow flickered across the carpet, maliciously intent on its macabre play. It gave up the burlesque of his actions and eagerly explored the room, darting from corner to corner, climbing the walls, scuttling over dusty shelves, burrowing under furniture. Now it appeared more intensely black, more solid, than ever before; its vitality was frightening.

Mr. Cardillo shuttered the windows; but the light, filtering through cracks he had never before noticed, revealed the hideous thing as it roved at will. He drew heavy curtains, blocked the crack under the door with newspapers. The room was dark, the air still, the shadow no longer visible.

Mr. Cardillo sat in a chair in utter blackness, unseeing, yet knowing his shadow was ever present, a dark form hovering over him, following his every movement with uncanny prescience. Sweat froze in tiny beads on his pale face; his hands were clammy and trembling.

The hours passed, and Mr. Cardillo sat unmoving in his chair. His body felt weak, his eyes heavy with lack of sleep, his face lined with fear. The room was cold, and he knew the sun had gone down and it was night-black outside. Still he lit no lamp; he was afraid to see that flickering, effervescent thing which had once been his shadow. He knew it was still with him, could feel its aura of power grow stronger as he weakened, as if it were draining the life-force from um, feeding on him in some vampiric way.

He could feel it tugging at his inkles, trying to pull him out of the chair; it wanted to go out into the moonlight, back to the cemetery and the newly dug grave. The tugging was insistent; Mr. Cardillo could only keep his legs from moving by holding them down with his hands; his feet tapped an odd rhythm on the carpet

The very darkness became oppressive, seemed to close in about him, stifling him. A dreadful coldness saturated him, numbing his arms; his body stiffened and only his legs moved with restless urgency, forcing him upright, carrying him towards the door.

Mr. Cardillo wrestled with the lock, opened the door and went on to the porch. Silver-pale moonlight glittered on the cypress trees in the cemetery. His shadow ran eagerly forward, black and strong and full-bodied, dancing with wild abandon, revelling in the knowledge of its triumph. With shuddering hands and leaden face, Mr. Cardillo opened the gate of the cemetery and passed inside.

His shadow darted like an arrow for the empty grave—*and Mr. Cardillo followed....*

A LITTLE NIGHT FISHING

"Here is a gale warning. Sea areas Sole and Fastnet. Force eight, imminent."

Robson switched off the wheelhouse radio and stepped on to the deck. The sky was clear and the sea calm. Well, the weathermen had been known to be wrong before, but there was no harm in checking with the locals. Not that it mattered; he had to go out tonight whatever the weather. Big Todd was not a man to accept excuses.

He studied the appearance of the cruiser before he left: everything looked all right, the fishing tackle was prominently displayed. He crossed the gangplank to the jetty and headed towards the Black Swan.

Robson was a heavy man with a perpetual scowl, dressed in roll-neck sweater, jeans and rope-soled shoes. He didn't like the sea or boats, he didn't like being away from the Smoke—but he liked the money.

Tregorrow, on the Cornish coast, was a scattering of grey stone houses, a small harbour and a pub. He crossed the quay in quick strides and went inside.

Four blue-jerseyed fishermen sat at a table with cards and a crib-board. A giant of a man stood watching them. Behind the bar, the publican's wife polished glasses.

"Pint of bitter," Robson called and, as the giant turned to look at him, added: "Join me?"

"Aye, I can sink a pint. I'm Fletch."

"Robbie."

A big hand surrounded one of the two mugs pushed across the counter. "Nice little boat you've got there, Robbie. Fast, I'd bet. You do a lot of fishing?"

"*Sweet Violet*? She's fast enough for what I want. I get my kicks night fishing—just an amateur, for sport, like."

"You'll need to watch this coastline," Fletch said in a warning tone.

"Yeah, more rocks than Hatton Garden. What d'you think to the weather just now?"

"Blowing up a storm, I'd reckon."

"What's a little storm?" Robson said, smiling. "Adds zest to the job, and *Sweet Violet* can take it."

Fletch didn't answer, just stared at the visitor, weighing him up.

Robson stared back. Fletch was blond with blue eyes, making him wonder if the Vikings had ever penetrated to this southwest corner of Britain. A big one, but he could take him. Robson was cockney and expert in the ways of backstreet fighting.

"We get some bad storms on this coast," Fletch said. "In the past, that made a living for the wreckers. They'd use false lights to lure a ship on to the rocks, then plunder it. None o' that now, of course—but we still get the storms."

He swallowed the rest of his pint and wiped the hairy back of a hand across his mouth. When he spoke again, his voice was soft, gentle almost.

"There's not so many wrecks now, either. Did you know this coast is haunted? 'Tis true as I stand at this bar—" His voice grew insistent. "Too many have seen the ghost not to believe. Some say 'tis the phantom of some poor sailor murdered by wreckers. Come a storm, and fishermen see the grey wraith waving a lantern and warning them away from the rock. Reckon it's saved a few lives."

"Yeah? A real live ghost?"

"No, this un's been dead a hundred years. And if you happen to see it tonight, you'll do well to take notice, Robbie."

* * * * * *

The sea had an oily swell when Robson put out. The sun was a ball of fire sinking below the horizon and gulls wheeled and screamed beneath scudding cloud. On the jetty, Fletch stood beside drying nets, watching. Robson waved casually but the Cornishman ignored him.

The hell with you, friend, Robson thought and gave all his attention to the cruiser. *Sweet Violet* moved along easily, driven by two one-hundred-horse-power diesels, her bow parting the sea like a knife. No sign of ships on the grey water. Good. The last thing he wanted was a customs cutter nosing around. Robson checked his watch and compass, watching the receding cliffs for landmarks. There'd be a moon on his way back and he didn't want any foul-up, not with Todd waiting in a fast car. He had to know exactly where the shoals and reefs lay.

He motored at a steady speed, timing distance on a set course for the rendezvous. A huge tanker passed slowly in the distance. The lights of land faded and he seemed alone on a great grey ocean.

The swell increased and a wind began to keen. The moon went behind storm clouds.

Presently, on time and in the right place, a fishing boat showed. As he closed with it, he read the name on the bow *Tante Marie*. He cruised parallel to the boat and a man in a beret flashed a torch: two short, pause, one long, repeated. Robson completed his half of the recognition signal and the Frenchman tossed a small package on a line to him. Robson caught it, cut the line and held up the packer to show he'd got it.

The two boats veered apart.

Robson placed the packet in a specially constructed compartment behind the chart locker and turned back for the English coast. That little packet was worth a few thou, but he never considered double-crossing Big Todd. Todd was the connection between a Paris mob specializing in jewel robberies and a fence in Hatton Garden. He also had a fancy way with a razor.

The French boat dropped from view as rain came gusting down. *Sweet Violet* began to rise and fall. At the wheel, Robson smiled. He wouldn't even have to pretend to catch fish now; the rising gale was a perfect excuse to run for harbour.

A dark sea merged with a dark sky and rain slanted down, effectively blocking any view he might have had. Mounting waves tossed the cruiser about like a cork; it was all Robson could do to stay on course. The wind howled and rain drummed on the wheelhouse roof.

He peered into the gloom with aching eyes, listening as waves slammed the hull like the blows of a sledgehammer. He studied his watch and compass, timing himself. By now he was closing the shore, a shore infested with granite crags and shoal water.

Now he heard it, above the wind and the rain, the noise of surf breaking over rocks. There was not a glimmer of light anywhere and he cursed. The black night was a shroud covering him.

He had difficulty keeping the boat headed where he wanted, staring with suspicion at the compass. He felt uneasy; he wasn't used to relying solely on instruments. If he didn't see the lights of land soon he would be in trouble.

The crash of breakers sounded ominously close and he struggled into a life-jacket. A hell of a time to wish he'd learnt to swim....

Water poured across the wheelhouse window, though whether it was rain or sea he couldn't tell. *Sweet Violet* pitched and tossed as wind and waves battered her.

Then, through the darkness, a weak light winked at him. Robson stared in concentration. Had he imagined it? No, there was a light, swinging crazily. It might have been an oil lamp. As he neared the pinpoint of yellow light, he saw a faint grey figure holding a lantern in one hand and swinging it to and fro.

The figure appeared to be a sailor in striped jersey, wearing a wool cap and standing atop a rock in the storming sea. It appeared so pale as to be unreal and did not look wet. Robson saw spray break over the figure...no, through it.

Paralysis gripped him. Sweat turned to ice. Fletch's ghost! He stared wild-eyed at the apparition with its swinging lantern, and trembled.

A ghostly voice lifted above the wind. "Rocks...rocks ahead."

Robson broke the grip of fear and wrenched desperately at the wheel, turning the cruiser away from the light. The hull juddered as she struck, throwing him off balance and he hit his head on the wall. He had a brief glimpse of a sharp-edged reef ripping along the hull, then water swirled at his feet.

In a daze, he scrambled through the doorway and clung to the deck-rail. An undertow caught the boat and swept her inshore. Robson clung to the rail, wet and cold, thinking of a fortune in diamonds hidden behind the chart locker. Big Todd would cut his heart out if he lost them—if he survived this.

Sweet Violet crashed against another rock, swung about and struck again. The wind hammered her, turning her over. Robson lost his grip and was washed overboard. He struggled weakly as his mouth filled with salt water. His feet touched bottom and he lurched upright, spluttering and gulping air.

The wind hurled him forward and he fell face down on wet sand. A wave rolled over him as he lay gasping like a stranded fish. He could make out the dark shape of the cruiser, wedged between jutting crags, some twenty yards away. Get the diamonds, he thought, get out of here—but his legs were lead weights. It was just too much effort to stand against the gale. Rest a moment, then he'd—

Shadowy figures gathered about him. One, closer than the others, stooped over him. He recognized the blond Viking from the pub.

"Fletch! Thank God, help me...."

Fletch stared down, unsmiling. "Still alive then, Robbie?" The giant selected a slab of rock and lifted it. "See our ghost, did thee? As I said, it's real enough—but I told one lie. 'Tis not the ghost of a drowned sailor, but of a wrecker. One of the Brethren. Aye, and it still lures boats on to the rocks for us!"

He brought down the rock, cracking Robson's skull as neat as slicing an egg.

ABOUT THE AUTHOR

Born in Brighton in 1920, and living most of his life in Kingston upon Thames, Surrey, SYDNEY JAMES BOUNDS, 86, died November 24, 2006, after battling cancer.

Bounds' first published short story was a supernatural tale, "Strange Portrait" in 1946, and he went on to sell hundreds of stories and forty-two novels in a lifetime of writing. He became a very successful children's writer, and appeared in dozens of junior magazines, annuals and anthologies. He also wrote more than two dozen comic book scripts. Alongside this work he published scores of adult dark fantasy and science fiction stories. His science fiction appeared in the US magazines *Other Worlds* and *Fantastic Universe,* and more widely in the UK, in *New Worlds, Science Fantasy, Authentic, Nebula,* the John Spencer paperback magazines, *Vision of Tomorrow,* and *Science Fiction Monthly.* Supernatural magazine appearances included *Fantasy Tales, Fantasy Annual* and other small press magazines, but most of his best supernatural tales appeared in the long series of ghost and horror anthologies published by Fontana, edited by Mary Danby and R. Chetwynd-Hayes. Particularly outstanding were "The Circus", which was adapted by George Romero for American TVs *Tales from the Dark Side*, and "The Mask," which was adapted for UK radio. A generous selection of the best of these stories is to be found in the two-volume collection, THE BEST OF SYDNEY J. BOUNDS (Wildside Press, 2002, edited by Philip Harbottle).

In recent years, along with science fiction, Bounds continued

to write new supernatural stories, appearing regularly in each issue of FANTASY ADVENTURES (Wildside Press, edited by Philip Harbottle.) His dark fantasy stories there included "Writer for Hire" (#2, 2002), "The Ballet of the Cats" (#3, 2003), "The Wall" (#5, 2003), "The Excavation" (#6, 2005), "The Trunk" (# 7, 2003), "Dreamboat" (#9, 2004), and "Victim" (#11, 2004). The final 13th issue of this magazine featured seven of his last stories. His horror story anthology appearances include "Homecoming" in MOONLIGHT ONLY (2002), "A Taste for Blood" in THE MAMMOTH BOOK OF VAMPIRES (2004), "The Circus" in THE MAMMOTH BOOK OF NEW TERROR (2004), and "The Night Comers" in GREAT GHOST STORIES (2004), and "A Little Night Fishing" in TALES TO FREEZE THE BLOOD (2006) all edited by Stephen Jones.

Bounds published more than forty novels, beginning with a detective thriller in 1950, A COFFIN FOR CLARA aka CARLA'S REVENGE, but soon switched to writing SF and westerns, most notably his "Savage" series, begun in 2000, with the eighth and last novel, SAVAGE RIDES WEST appearing posthumously in 2007. He also returned to writing detective novels, and amongst his later titles were THE CLEOPATRA SYNDICATE (1990 Italian, 2007 English), ENFORCER (2005), THE GIRL HUNTERS (2005), and BOOMERANG (2008).

Novels of SF interest include DIMENSION OF HORROR (1953), THE MOON RAIDERS (1955), THE WORLD WRECKER (1956), THE ROBOT BRAINS (1957), revised as MISSION OF THE BRAINS (2009), THE PREDATORS (1977 Italian, 2002 English), and STAR TRAIL (1978 Italian, 2003 English).

The best of Bounds' novels are set to be reprinted by the Borgo Press, beginning with THE WORLD WRECKER, together with some new posthumous SF novels

It has been a privilege for me to act as Bounds' agent, and occasionally, to collaborate with him. A recent highlight has been the conclusion of a deal for the sale of the film rights to one his best short stories ('The Animators', 1975) to a leading British

movie company, Qwerty Films. The film went into production in 2011, directed by Ruairi Robinson, with a screenplay by long-time Bounds fan Clive Dawson....

In addition to his own writing, Bounds worked as a Tutor for a Writing School for many years, and this was work he loved, encouraging and helping new authors to break into print. Just three days before he died, he learned of, and gave his blessing to, the inauguration of the "Best Newcomer—the Sydney J. Bounds Award" given annually by the British Fantasy Society.